AS THE UNDERWORLD TURNS

GOOD TO THE LAST DEMON, BOOK 1

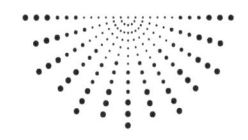

ROBYN PETERMAN

JOIN MY NEWSLETTER!

Copyright © 2022 by Robyn Peterman

All rights reserved.

No part of this book may be reproduced in any form or by any electronic or mechanical means, including information storage and retrieval systems, without written permission from the author, except for the use of brief quotations in a book review.

This book is a work of fiction. Names, characters, places, and incidents either are the product of the author's imagination or are used fictitiously. Any resemblance to actual persons, living or dead, businesses, companies, events, or locales is coincidental.

This book contains content that may not be suitable for young readers 17 and under.

Cover design by *Cookies Inc.*

Edited by *Kelli Collins*

ACKNOWLEDGMENTS

As The Underworld Turns is a spinoff of The Good To The Last Death Series. You do not have to have read the other series, but there are fun call outs for those who have. I do believe that Daisy and Gideon might make an appearance in this one.

I wrote The Facts of Midlife knowing I was going to spin Abaddon off into his own series.
And then I came up with the perfect heroine.

I promised myself a very long time ago that someday I would write a story about an actress and use some of my real life experiences…
That time has come. LOL
The names have been changed to protect the innocent and the guilty.

The situations have been slightly altered.
Clearly, I'm not a Demon—well not on a daily basis.

Cecily, our new and fabulous heroine, is a Demon.

So get ready for a wild, wild ride. I had a blast writing As The Underworld Turns and hope you love reading about Abaddon and Cecily.

As always, writing may be a solitary sport, but it takes a bunch of terrific people to get a book out into the world.

Renee — Thank you for my beautiful cover and for being the best badass critique partner in the world. TMB. LOL

Kelli — Your editing makes me look like a better writer. Thank you.

Wanda — You are the freaking bomb. Love you to the moon and back.

Heather, Nancy, Susan and Wanda — Thank you for reading early and helping me find the booboos. You all rock.

My Readers — Thank you for loving the stories that come from my warped mind. It thrills me.

Steve, Henry and Audrey — Your love and support makes all of this so much more fun. I love you people endlessly.

DEDICATION

For my readers. I can only hope I bring you as much happiness as you bring me.

MORE IN THE GOOD TO THE LAST DEMON SERIES

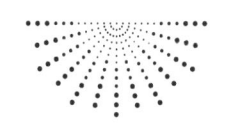

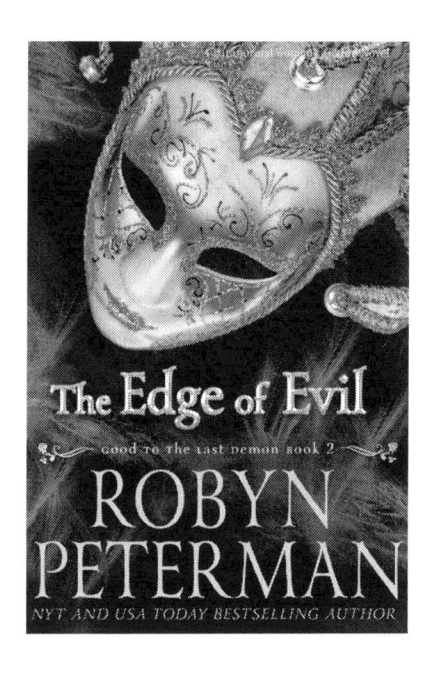

PREORDER BOOK TWO NOW!

BOOK DESCRIPTION

AS THE UNDERWORLD TURNS

What does a forty-year-old former child star do when she finds out she's a Demon?
A sitcom, of course.

Age is just a number unless you're an actress of a certain age trying to make a comeback in La La Land. Back in the day, I was the child star of the hit show *Camp Bites*. Today, I'm still living it down.

After a disastrous soap opera audition and getting fired from a TV show for not having a bodacious enough backside, one would think I'd be smart enough to go into real estate.

Nope.

Just found out from the rudest, meanest, and hottest guy alive that I'm a Demon. The jerk, also a Demon, goes by the name Abaddon—Abe to his friends.

I call him Dick.

He's come from the Underworld to protect me—insert laugh track—since there's a bounty on my head. Dick is not a welcome addition to my midlife madness. However, he won't go away, and now, he's my new boss.

Fine. Whatever. All I ever wanted to do in my life was pretend. I can pretend to get along with Dick. I can pretend that I'm not wildly attracted to him. Not sure I can pretend I'm human anymore, or that a supernatural assassin isn't trying to cancel me, but I'm going to fake it until I make it. Or I get killed.

As the Underworld turns upside down, so have the days of my life.

***The Good To The Last Demon Series is a spinoff of the Good To The Last Death Series.

PROLOGUE

A day in the life of a somewhat desperate actress...
Three months earlier

Eighth callback.

For a soap.

I checked for lipstick on my teeth for the umpteenth time. The amount of gloss I'd slapped on made me feel slimy. My lips felt like they weighed ten pounds. But when in Rome...

The waiting room was filled with gals half my age. At forty, I was considered over-the-hill, but I'd somehow made it this far in the search for the newest character on the hit soap opera, *The Ocean is Deeply Moving*. "What am I doing here?" I muttered to myself. I didn't like soaps. I didn't watch soaps. I also didn't have a job at the moment.

"Hi! I'm Rhoda Spark!" a prepubescent, large-bosomed, bright-eyed and bushy-tailed youngster to my left said.

"I'm Cecily Bloom," I replied, wishing I was invisible. Making small talk while internally debating why I'd even shown up was distracting.

"I know!" she gushed. "You're amazing. Loved you in *Camp Bite*!"

Rhoda wore a mini-skirt that revealed her barely there pink panties. Her extremely low-cut crop top was obscene. Making eye contact was difficult, due to the fact I was pretty sure one of her nips had popped out. Again, I wanted to slap my own face for being here. However, I was a very polite former child star. Ending up in the rags for being mean to a fan—even if we were competing for the same crappy job—wasn't my thing.

"Thank you," I said, doing my best not to reach over and pull her shirt up. The nip slip was most likely on purpose. Who was I to fix her game? Maybe it worked for her.

"Watched it religiously when I was in the first grade!" she squealed.

My smile felt brittle on my lips. I'd just been bitch-slapped by a teenager named Rhoda with an exposed boob. Awesome.

I'd told my agent numerous times that I didn't want to do daytime TV. However, here I was. I had no one to blame but myself. I'd accepted the audition. And with each callback, I'd started to want the job. It didn't even matter that the character was named Bambi "Boo" Blakely—a neurosurgeon who wore six-inch heels and baked pies for the poor in her off time. Not to mention, the ghost of her ex-husband still lived with her.

Nope. My need to win outweighed my good judgement and taste by a long shot.

One by one, the gals went into the room to read the stomach-churning scene about how difficult it was to be taken seriously as a sexy neurosurgeon who had metaphysical and aerobic sex with a ghost. The dialogue was absurd. I'd rewritten it so I didn't erupt into hysterical laughter when I read it aloud. That might have been why I'd been called back.

I was the only actress who hadn't sounded like a freaking idiot.

One by one, each of them was dismissed. Some left pissed. Some exited in tears. Rhoda, the Nip Slip gal, was devastated. I'd almost told her she might not want to expose herself at her next audition, but she was gone so fast I missed the opportunity. The only actress left was the one currently in the room and me.

The fact that I could book the job was horrifying. The fact that I might not was terrifying. My warring instincts told me to run while there was still time. My need to win insisted I stay. The reality that there were multiple conversations going on in my head was an indicator that I'd lost my mind. I wasn't sure which voice to listen to. They were all loud.

Maybe I'd missed my calling in show business. I was one hell of a script doctor. However, the magic for me was in front of the camera. Hence, I was at the eighth callback for a piece of junk.

"They're ready to see you, Cecily," the five-foot-nothing casting director said, examining me with obvious dismay.

"What?" I asked, alarmed. Had I spilled something on my clothes? Shit. That would suck. I'd dressed with care. My skirt was so tight, one could probably see my religion and the blouse was low cut—not nip-slip low, but low enough for a bit of cleavage—perfect for a surgeon who wore Jimmy Choos to operate. I knew from the last callback that there would be at least forty people in the room listening to me wax poetic about brain tumors and pecan pie. "Is there something wrong with my shirt?"

"It's not the shirt, it's what's in it… or rather, what's not in it," she muttered as she opened the door and ushered me in.

What in the ever-loving hell did she mean by that? While

my rack was nice, it wasn't necessarily *soap opera nice*, so I'd stuffed my bra with damned silicone chicken cutlets for the ridiculous audition. I hated the rubbery boob enhancers, and I was suffering massive under-boob sweat to make my girls look bigger. What more could she want?

"And lastly, we have Cecily Bloom," the bitchy miniature woman announced.

The smiles from the group were polite but unenthused. I didn't know why until I did...

"Thank you!" a blonde bombshell squealed as she blew kisses to the network suits. "I just loved reading for you today. I really feel Bambi 'Boo' Blakely deeply in my ample chest!"

The smiles perked up... especially the male ones. Why was I here if she was still auditioning?

The busty actress couldn't have been more than twenty. How she could have gotten through medical school and become a world-renowned neurosurgeon who baked was beyond me, but looking for sound reasoning in the world of smoke and mirrors was counterproductive. The show was called *The Ocean is Deeply Moving*. What did I expect?

"I can wait in the lobby if you're not ready for me," I said with a smile that I prayed didn't look seriously constipated.

"No," a stern-looking woman in a purple power suit said. "We want to do a side by side with you and Ophelia."

"Awesome!" Ophelia screamed, bouncing up and down like she'd just won the big showcase on *The Price is Right*.

She probably wasn't old enough to remember *The Price is Right*.

Run, my inner voice bellowed. I closed my eyes for a brief moment then plastered a wide smile on my face. "Sounds great."

My inner voice split right in half like Rumpelstiltskin. She

AS THE UNDERWORLD TURNS

was pissed at me. I didn't blame her, but it would be mortifying to walk out now. I was a pro. I'd been a pro since I was a kid. Walking to the center of the room, I took my place next to Ophelia. It was wrong of me to judge her on the size of her knockers. She might be a lovely person.

"Get ready to go down, bitch," she muttered under her breath.

She was not a lovely person.

Her bright white toothy smile was still enormous. Her lips didn't move. "I'm Bambi 'Boo' Blakely. No one is going to get in my way—especially not some washed-up, freak-of-nature, ancient child star. I'm done with you messing with my life."

Harsh.

However, Ophelia did have some talent. She was an incredible ventriloquist and a colossal bitch. I might be a washed-up child star, but I was not ancient or a freak of nature. And as for messing with her life, I'd never laid eyes on her until today. Ophelia needed some therapy and possibly a straightjacket.

"Please stand back-to-back," the casting director said.

This was not happening. "Do you need me to read the sides?" I asked politely.

"No," the purple-suited exec chimed in. "We already know what an incredible actress you are, Cecily. We just need to decide if you're attractive enough."

"I'm sorry, what?" I asked, feeling like I might puke. The giggle from the tits on my right didn't help.

"Ohhh, don't get me wrong," Purple Lady said. "You're a beautiful woman. We're just not sure if you're soap opera beautiful. The conundrum for us is that your reading was brilliant."

"Yes," an exec with what I could only describe as a porn-stache added. "It's a real quandary if we're going to err on the side of talent or tits."

Why hadn't I listened to my inner voice? She was smarter than me. Way smarter.

"Let me help you out with that," I said, finding my lady balls. I didn't need the money. I had plenty of that. It was about the work. This was not the work I wanted to do. "I think tits will sell better than talent. I can't really see myself humping a ghost in the breakroom at the hospital. Whereas I could easily picture Ophelia humping practically anything anywhere." My inner voice quit having a meltdown. I took that as a good sign.

"She has a point," Porn-stache said as the rest of the dumbasses in the room nodded their agreement.

"Yes!" Ophelia announced triumphantly. "I can hump like a pro."

I rolled my eyes. "I'm sure you've had lots of practice," I told her sweetly. She looked wildly confused. It was a nice moment. "So, on that unappetizing note, I'd like to say thank you for considering me, but I'll have to pass. I firmly believe that Ophelia is the humper with tits you're searching for—not me. She will elevate the show to dizzying heights."

"What she said," Ophelia squealed.

"I have an idea," Porn-stache bellowed, jumping to his feet and pumping his fists over his head. "Cecily, would you be willing to play Ophelia's mother? It would be a slam dunk—tits *and* talent."

The room full of execs broke out into applause. Ophelia bowed. This was like an episode of *Punk'd* on crack, except it was real—very sadly and unfortunately real.

"Umm… no," I said. "But again, thank you. Have a great life, everyone! Good luck, Ophelia. I have a feeling you might need it."

Porn-stache looked crestfallen. I wanted to kick him in the nuts. That would be a bad move. Might feel great in the moment, but would be unwise in the long game. Unsure how much more humiliation I could handle, I made a quick exit.

I snot-cried for an hour when I got home. The magic was almost gone. If there were any more days like today, I was done with the business of show.

CHAPTER ONE

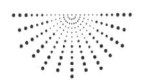

Three months later.

Age is just a number…

Well, not if you're an actress of a certain age in La La Land trying to make a comeback.

"For the love of everything I don't have time for," I muttered staring with dismay at my reflection in the mirror. "Well, I suppose life could be far worse." At least I wasn't on *The Ocean is Deeply Moving*.

Life *was* getting better. Soaps were out. Episodic TV was now the name of the game.

Ophelia did indeed get the role of Bambi "Boo" Blakely on *The Ocean is Deeply Moving*. Her reviews were scathing and rumor had it she was going to be bludgeoned by her ghostly ex any day now. That entire situation was a bullet thankfully dodged. Although, Porn-stache had called my agent and made an offer for me to play Selina Songbird—an aging jazz singer who read tea leaves for strangers and fostered lab mice. Needless to say, it was a hard pass.

After all these years, I was still trying to live down *Camp*

Bite. I didn't need to add *The Ocean is Deeply Moving* to my list of questionable choices.

I avoided looking at the iris of my left eye. It was freakish, and I'd worn a contact to cover it as far back as I could recall. My dad affectionately called it my Goat Eye. I didn't feel a whole lot of affection for the horizontal, glowing silver line that should have been circular. It was a birth defect—one that there was no way of fixing. Believe me, I'd tried.

Popping in the sapphire-blue contact lens that matched my normal eye, I moved closer to the mirror and scrunched my nose. The fine lines weren't too bad for real life, but in TV Land, under the harsh and unforgiving eye of the camera lens, it wasn't going to cut it. "Maybe it's time to make a date with Botox."

"It would certainly be an improvement over the last rascal you danced the horizontal tango with, Cecily."

I screamed, startled by the disembodied voice. I snatched up the first thing my hand touched, a tube of toothpaste, and held it like a gun—squeeze and shoot. Blinding an intruder with Crest might give me the precious seconds I needed to run for my life… or not.

Before I could shoot my shot, I noticed my brother Sean sitting in the lotus position on the floor of my bathroom. I hadn't even realized he was in the same room with me. My self-preservation instincts were sorely lacking. The eye lash curler would have been a better weapon choice, but I'd been in a hurry. Getting lost in my thoughts was going to land me six feet under one of these days. Sean could have been a demented serial killer or a ballsy Jehovah's witness.

"Oh my God, you're an asshat," I told him, swatting his head.

My six-foot-one younger and only brother was wearing my

bathrobe and possibly my underwear. He was averse to doing laundry and tended to pilfer anything that was 100% organic cotton and clean. I wasn't short by any stretch of the imagination at five-foot-nine, but he looked ridiculous in the ill-fitted pink terrycloth. If he was wearing my panties, I was sure his thirty-eight-year-old junk wasn't faring too well.

"Better than an asshole," he shot back with a chuckle.

"Not much," I pointed out, trying not to grin. My lips tilted up and the smile won out.

Unfortunately, my brother was correct in his assessment of my paramours. I'd kissed a lot of frogs over the years. I'd even been married for three months back in my twenties to a narcissistic idiot and preferred to block out that section of my life. Hindsight was 20/20 no matter what the shape of your pupil happened to be. The idiot, Slash Gordon—and yes, that was his given name—had gone on to become a rock star in a hair band. I was definitely not one of his groupies.

I'd freely admit I didn't have the best taste in *banging partners*. But then again, neither did my brother or my dad. We had a family history of making shitty choices in the romance department. Sean had been engaged too many times to count. Thankfully, he'd never made it to the altar. He'd made it down the aisle twice, but pulled a Julia Roberts runaway bride move both times. Not a good look for anyone. I loved my brother, but he wasn't exactly responsible husband material. He was more of a very pretty man-child.

And my dad… he'd married my mom, who'd deserted us the day I was born, then followed that failed relationship with nuptials to Sean's mom, who had also hit the road pretty quick. Bill Jackson Bloom—BJ to his buddies—had singlehandedly raised two kids with a ton of love, cereal for dinner and regular therapy for all. My dad was a distracted mess of profound wisdom, horrible cooking skills, a time management deficit, and he gave the best bear hugs in the Universe. He was a keeper.

"Seriously though, I don't think you should have Botulism injected into your face," Sean said, putting one foot over his head and behind his neck. He was wearing my favorite green panties.

I rolled my eyes. "That's priceless coming from you, dude."

"The herbs I imbibe are natural—Mother Earth's medicinal magic," he reminded me, putting the other foot over his head. My brother resembled a human pretzel in pink terrycloth with hairy legs.

I ignored him and went back to studying my face.

While the fine lines around my eyes weren't hideous, they weren't welcome. The rest of my forty-year-old self had held up pretty well—boobs were still perky with the help of sturdy underwire, weight was acceptable for my height due to running six miles a day and giving up sugar, along with my beloved bread and pasta. No silver wisdom sparkles yet in my shoulder-length, jet-black hair. I didn't sell insurance. I didn't sell shoes. The wares I sold were my creativity, my face and my talent. Basically, I sold my soul on a daily basis.

Well, that was a little dramatic, but the truth was a bitch.

"Can I make a suggestion?" Sean asked.

"Nope."

"Excellent," he replied, reaching into the pocket of the robe and producing a wad of sticky gummies. The fact that he could find the pocket while tied in a human knot was impressive. "If you ingest one and a half of these, you won't be able to see the laugh lines, or much of anything for that matter. We can go to the airport, lay on the hood of my car and watch the underside of planes as they take off and land. I'm working on a new poem about the disappearing ozone layer. The theme is the noxious stench of fossil fuel."

"While that sounds like an outstanding way to waste a few hours of my life that I can't get back, I'll have to pass," I said with an amused shake of my head. "I have to actually work so you can sit on your stoned butt and compose life-altering poetry."

He grinned and saluted me. I laughed. He was a hot mess and I adored him. As strange as my only sibling was, he was also a world-renowned poet. He didn't make much of an income but he had legions of rabid and probably stoned fans. I couldn't make heads or tails of his non-linear verse, but he'd explained that one had to indulge in jazz cabbage—his favorite term for pot—to fully savor his creative genius. My guess was that meant there were tons of people in the world who were enjoying the Devil's Lettuce regularly—Sean's second-favorite term for Mary Jane.

I squinted at one of the people who I loved most for a long beat then proceeded to slap on some war paint to camouflage my eye crinklies. "Why are you in my house at seven in the morning? Your eyes don't usually open before noon."

Sean sighed dramatically and popped a gummy into his mouth. "Dad is lacquering the cockroach. The smell is debilitating. Pretty sure I lost a few brain cells before I crawled over on my hands and knees to your house."

Since we lived next door to each other, he hadn't had far to crawl. It was a gross exaggeration to say I needed to earn money to support my brother's jazz cabbage habit. As young children, both Sean and I had starred in a sitcom together for eight years—*Camp Bite*. We'd played vampire siblings pre-*Twilight*—fangs and all. It was every kind of cheesy, and I was still living it down to this day. However, I had a really nice house, no debt and a kickass extended-cab pickup truck named Judy because of my fake blood-sucking youth. One of Sean's side gigs was playing the stock market. He'd made our money make money even *jazz-cabbaged* out of his mind.

Our dad had refused to touch a cent of our childhood earnings and invested for us wisely. We had no clue of the fortunes we'd amassed until our teens. We'd grown up well-loved in a middleclass, three-bedroom home in the Valley. We'd lived frugally on the income of a sporadically employed art teacher who painted houses on the side while creating masterpieces that didn't sell in our garage.

Once we realized we had some coin, we'd purchased two beautiful Craftsman bungalows next to each other on a quaint and quiet street in Venice. Lemon trees and twisting hot pink bougainvillea vines along with the orange and avocado trees had sold me on the property. Being close to the ocean was a big plus too.

I loved to stand at the water's edge in the middle of the night and talk to the stars. Occasionally, I would sing. It was the only place I could belt one out without rupturing anyone's eardrums. To say I was tone deaf would be an understatement. The fish were just fine with my off-key version of *Les Misérables*.

Dad wouldn't let us buy him a house. He was adamant that our money was our money. So, we'd tricked him into living with Sean. My not-so-brilliant brother had pretended to go blind for an entire six months. It was a shitshow of pratfalls and a few broken bones. He'd gone method and had been very committed to the role. The fact that he was still able to drive during his time of sightlessness had been the only real kink into the believability of his performance.

Dad, being a good sport and incredibly sick of Sean snapping his femur, agreed to move in. That had been fifteen years ago and it suited us to a T.

Life had been pretty perfect, and I wouldn't have changed a thing about my childhood—even the fact that we didn't go to normal school or do normal kid things because of the TV show. I didn't need a mother and neither did Sean. We had a dad who had been there through the happy, sad and wonderful times. We called him Man-mom or BJ. I tended to go with Man-mom since BJ had dual meanings. It was hard to keep a straight face while referring to one's paternal unit as an oral sex maneuver, or as Sean would say, slurpin' the gherkin.

"Don't think you need to inhale lacquer to lose brain cells," I commented with a raised brow as I expertly swiped on mascara. "Is Dad literally putting shellac on a cockroach?"

I was an actress. Sean was a poet. Dad was retired now, but fancied himself a multimedia artist. He always had a project going and it was usually alarming.

"Technically, no," Sean said, untangling himself from his position and hopping to his feet. "It's a thirty-by-thirty-foot painting of a cockroach riding a unicycle along the River Styx."

I winced and pressed the bridge of my nose. "Jesus," I muttered. "Man-mom's obsession with Hell is getting a little out of hand."

"Possibly," Sean agreed, picking up my toothbrush and using it. "But it's better than the one of Bozo the Clown juggling miniature hellhounds as that skeleton dude, Charon, offers him a ferry ride into Hell."

My mouth fell open. "I missed that one."

"It was epic," Sean said with a mouthful of toothpaste. "BJ was feeling it."

I mentioned nothing about the gross fact that my toothbrush was in his mouth. I'd toss it or dip it in the toilet and leave it until he used it again… which he would.

"Do you think he's okay?" I asked. Man-mom had been creating pieces with an Underworld theme for a few years now. Shockingly, they seemed to sell. I had no clue who wanted the decoupaged, life-size vase of Dolly Parton and Ron Howard playing poker with the Devil, but since it was no longer on the front porch, I could only assume it was now in someone's collection.

"He's fine," Sean assured me. "Do you have any decaffeinated coffee?"

I gagged. "There is no sane reason in the world for decaffeinated coffee."

"I'm taking that as a no," he said with a lopsided grin.

"Correct."

Sean was stupidly handsome, as was Man-mom. I was easy on the eyes as well. It was rough for women of a certain age in Hollywood, but if you had good genes it helped. I was far prouder of my talent and work ethic than my looks. Looks faded with time. Big balls, thick skin and strength of character lasted forever.

"Do you ever miss acting?" I asked my brother as I pushed him out of the bathroom so I could get dressed.

"Nope." He gnashed his teeth like they were fangs in memory of *Camp Bite*. "Not a bit."

I tilted my head to the side and laughed. "You were really good. The possibilities would have been endless."

He laughed. "I was *good* when I was ten and playing an undead character who glowed in the dark," he reminded me. "Plus, if everything is possible, then nothing is true."

On those profound yet confusing words, he made his way to my kitchen to pilfer some breakfast.

"If you eat the blueberry bagel, you die," I called after him.

"Thought you gave up bread," he yelled back.

"Shit. You're right," I said with a groan. "Eat the bagel and the donuts, please."

"On it."

He was a very good brother. Saving me from myself was hard work.

CHAPTER TWO

"Run-through for network in ten," the stage manager called out.

I closed my eyes and took a deep, calming breath. My nerves were acceptable. Nervousness meant I cared, or that was the story I was going with. I hadn't worked in a while. The show, *Family Spies*, was a typical sitcom. No biggie. The fact that it was the network's top-rated series made it kind of a biggie.

"Ten minutes," I muttered under my breath. "No problem. Like riding a bike." I hoped.

The cavernous soundstage was comfortingly familiar. It was the very same stage where I'd worked for eight years straight in my long-lost youth. I was sure my name was still carved under the makeup table in dressing room A. However, dressing room A was for stars. I was not the star of this show. My name was last on the call sheet. How the once mighty had fallen…

A job was a job.

Half of the set was dressed to look like the interior of an

upper-middle-class living room on the tacky side, complete with an over-the-top chandelier and bar. The furniture was a little stuffy and formal, but the color theme killed that dead. Bright yellow and purple mixed with neon green assaulted my eyes. Hopefully on camera it looked better than it did in person. The other half of the set looked like a Podunk country store filled with every kind of cheese known to man—also with the same color theme.

"Nasty," I whispered to myself.

"And then some," a voice behind me agreed.

Slapping my hand over my mouth, I whipped around then heaved a massive sigh of relief. It was my longtime buddy, Jenni Gallagher.

Jenni had been on *Camp Bite* with Sean and me back in the day. She'd played our bubbly human cohort who found all the clues for our undead missions. Jenni was ten years older and a whole lot smarter in the scheme of life. After the show ended, she'd left the acting game, gone to cosmetology school and was now a top-notch makeup artist in the biz. She was small in stature, sexily plump with an insanely cool silver streak in the front of her wild red hair.

"Dude," I said, hugging her. "I thought I got busted."

She grinned. "You did," Jenni replied, studying my face. "Did you get filler?"

"No." I touched my cheeks. "Do I need it?"

She shook her head. "Nope. Your skin is like a baby's butt. Gals pay the big bucks to look like you, my friend."

I laughed. "You lie like a rug."

"True," she shot back with a shrug. "But not today. You really look terrific, Cecily."

I wanted to kiss her. "God, you have no clue how much of a

relief it is to hear you say that. I had a come to Jesus with my crow's feet this morning."

"Laugh lines," she corrected me. "Well-earned happy crinkles."

"Sounds a lot better than grumpy grooves."

A laugh burst from Jenni's lips. "I'm gonna steal that one."

"It's yours," I told her. "I'm nervous."

She looked at me for a long moment. "Nerves are good. Means you care. It's when you no longer get the tingles before a run-through or a taping that you need to haul ass out of this shitty business."

Her words hit me in an odd place. "Is that why you left? No more tingles?"

Jenni shook her head. "Nope. When *Camp Bite* ended, I was an overweight late twenty-something-year-old gal whose catch phrase was 'Holy moly! What would Dracula do?' Kinda hard to find work. You feel me?"

I winced and giggled. It was a seriously bad legacy to leave behind.

"Anyhoo," she went on. "I'm a whole lot happier behind the scenes. I'm never out of work and I still get to be part of the magic."

Jenni had hit the nail on the head. I'd searched and searched for something else that would make me feel the magic and I'd never found it. Granted, the magic had become watered down over the years, but it was still there.

I noticed the crew nervously prepping for the run-through. "Is this a fun show to work on?"

So far, my feelings were mixed. I was on day three of the job and the star of the sitcom hadn't shown up yet. Apparently, he didn't believe in rehearsing. Cue eyeroll. Jonny Benji Runky liked to improv. He was a stand-up comic who'd scored a TV deal. I was warned to stay on my toes and go with whatever the overblown egomaniac did. There was a terror in the air that didn't bode well.

Jenni's lips compressed into a thin line. "This one's a paycheck," she said quietly, glancing around to make sure no one had overheard.

I nodded and sucked in a deep breath. My *tingles* were turning into cramps. Was I nuts to still be on the acting side of the business? Probably. At my age, a gal had to be crazy to keep on keeping on. Problem was, I wasn't qualified to do anything else. And on top of that, I still felt the passion for pretending.

"Just be you and do your thing, Cecily," Jenni said, checking her texts. "You have the magic that can't be taught—always have. Use and abuse. Gotta fix some lash extensions. See you on the flip side."

"Lunch soon?" I called out as she hustled to the makeup room.

"It's a date!"

The set was bustling. Shortly, the cast would wander out along with about twenty or so network executives—all of whom had opinions about everything. I had no clue how anything actually got done in the business of TV.

Not my problem. I was simply a hired gun for a short period of time. I just hoped Jonny Benji Runky showed up. It would be difficult to do a scene without a partner.

Inhaling deeply again, I tried to calm my nerves. The *nasty* hunks of cheese made my stomach growl since I'd only had a banana for breakfast. I'd watched my brother down my blueberry bagel and donuts and almost attacked him. Being carb deprived wasn't working well with my impulse control. However, the cheese was not an option. It might look tasty, but set food was covered in Vaseline, magic marker and hairspray. I'd rather eat cardboard than the cheddar on the counter.

"Five minutes," the stage manager announced.

The butterflies in my stomach morphed into a kick-line that made me slightly nauseous. What the heck was wrong with me? I'd done this since I was a kid. Jenni said I still had the magic. I chose to believe her. Granted, for the last decade or so I'd been doing informercials and crappy small parts in what I would generously call embarrassingly bad B movies... but I was still an actress. A mostly working actress. Even though some of the jobs I'd booked sucked, I didn't suck in them. Sean and Man-mom were very honest critics. The informercial I did hawking lawnmowers that doubled as sprinklers was a huge hit with Man-mom and Sean.

Not to mention, I'd been smart enough not to land my ass on *The Ocean is Deeply Moving* playing the mother of Ophelia with the size-D bosom.

I was a grownup child actor who hadn't become a statistic or snorted her income up her nose, leaving a trail of ex-husbands and appalling tabloid stories in my wake, and I hadn't had to resort to reality television to stay relevant.

I called that a win. Hurray for me.

Even so, being a forty-year-old semi-has-been, trying to make a comeback on a mega-hit TV sitcom was eating away at my self-confidence. Personally, I thought the show, *Family Spies,* stunk and Jonny Benji Runky stunk in it. But work was work.

The premise of *Family Spies* was almost as cringeworthy as *Camp Bite*... almost. It was difficult to top brother and sister bloodsuckers who went to human school by day and solved the woes of the mystical Underworld by night along with their trusty manservant Scotty, an eight-foot gargoyle shifter. Of course, Scotty had lived under our bunkbeds and could only be called to help when Sean and I gnashed our fangs and Hula-Hooped in unison. The canned laugh-track made each episode even more stomach-churning.

Although, as cheesy as it was, Sean and I had a blast doing it. The fact that it ran for eight years was a testament to the unsavory truth that the studio head's not-so-secret mistress played our clueless human mom. That hadn't ended well.

When the cat clawed its way out of the bag, the studio head's marriage bit the dust along with *Camp Bite*. Scarily, the show could be streamed now, and it had a cultish following. Hence, I was starting to get offers in better projects…like *Family Spies,* a sitcom about a family of idiots from Wisconsin who sold cheese by day and solved mysteries when they weren't selling cheese.

"Creativity is dead," I muttered.

"Sorry, missed that," the stage manager said, running around like a chicken with his head cut off. "You need something?"

I blanched then smiled politely. "Nope. I'm good. Just waiting to get started."

"Two minutes," he said, then jogged away to chat with the lighting crew.

"I can do this," I said as the execs filed in. Some were familiar. Some were so young they could have been my children.

My agent, Beyonce, had literally cried when I'd been offered the eight-episode arc on *Family Spies*. Her name wasn't Beyonce. No one was clear on what her real name was… including her. I'd signed with her ten years ago on the promise she would never send me out on any commercials involving sexually transmitted diseases, tampons, toilet paper, diarrhea or douche. So far, so good. Last month, Beyonce's name was

Madonna and the month before it was Gaga. She had a thing for female pop stars and legally changed her name on the regular. Most days I thought Beyonce had more lipliner than sense, but she was funny and a shark in negotiations.

Eight episodes on a hit show should have made me ecstatic. I was simply concerned—especially about the script. The role had called for a gal with a big bottom—as in a JLo booty. I didn't have a big bottom but had made the showrunners laugh their heads off during my audition. At forty, I was still doing damn good in the midlife body department. Of course, in Hollywood, forty might as well be eighty. Back in the day I could have shaved about ten years off my age and no one would have been the wiser, but with the dawn of the internet, fudging my time on Earth was impossible.

While I was honestly thrilled to have the job, the writers hadn't rewritten the part for a normal-assed gal. I assumed they would pad my rear end to make it *bootylicious*—their words, not mine. So far, no fake butt had been provided.

"You good, Cecily?" the wardrobe mistress asked, carrying a pile of coats and hats to use as set dressing.

Her name was Sushi—just Sushi. Pretty sure it wasn't the name she was born with, but who was I to judge? I'd worked with Sushi a bunch over the years. The woman was a very well-preserved sixty, blunt and all business, who enjoyed wearing low-cut tops that showed off her enviable assets. Sushi made it work. In her youth she must have been beautiful. What she lacked in the social graces department, she made up for in talent, professionalism and a sarcastic sense of humor.

A familiar face was a wonderful thing. "Not really," I admitted. "Have you seen a random ass floating around?"

She grinned. "Last I checked most of the people here were asses. Did you have a particular ass in mind?"

"I'm speaking literally," I told her. "My character is supposed to have a Kim Kardashian backside. I'm a little lacking in that department."

Sushi looked at my butt and nodded. "Don't worry about it. It's not an actual dress rehearsal per se."

I squinted at her. "Why am I in my costume then?" I asked, looking down in horror at the buttoned-up, eggplant-colored business suit paired with an overly starched white ruffled blouse and sensible shoes that had been in my dressing room when I'd arrived. It was butt ugly, but costars had very little input. Looking like an idiot was part of the game. I supposed I was lucky I was dressed at all. The last job I was on required me to be in a freaking bathing suit in thirty-degree weather for a week.

"I don't know why you're in costume," she said, glancing over her shoulder at the incoming cast. "No one else is."

"Shit," I mumbled, wanting to die. If someone thought these were my street clothes, I'd crap. "Do I have time to change?"

"Places," the stage manager called. "Top of show."

"Nope," Sushi said with a wince. "Just own it. You're gorgeous even in that hot mess."

"Not helping," I said, moving briskly to the area featuring the cheese store.

I felt a pair of hostile eyes on me. I looked around, half expecting it to be Jonny Benji Runky. Thankfully, it wasn't. That would have made today tremendously painful. Jonny Benji Runky was being fussed over by a gaggle of zealous network sycophants. The eyes didn't belong to the star of the show.

Nope. Instead, the owner of the vicious glare was probably the best-looking man I'd ever seen in my life. Around forty-five or close to it, he stood well over six feet tall and wasn't gushing over the improv idiot. His arms were crossed over his chest, and he'd placed himself on the outside of the fawning circle of kiss-ass network folk. His hair was as dark as mine and he wore it slightly too long. It was messy and sexy. His lips were ridiculous, and I thought his eyes were blue. Since they were narrowed to slits, I couldn't be sure. The black suit on his muscular body was expensive and he wore it well.

Was he an exec?

Shit.

"What the heck?" I muttered, looking around me to see if the man's scowl was intended for someone else. I'd never seen the rude jerk in my life.

Nope. I was standing solo. Did he hate *Camp Bite*? I mean, that was a possibility, but a weird one. Was he put out that I wasn't bootylicious? Was he offended by my ruffled shirt?

Whatever.

Hopefully, the dagger-staring dude wouldn't be my problem. I had enough of those right now.

CHAPTER THREE

"Places," the first assistant director called out again.

I went to my mark and hoped to hell and back that Jonny Benji Runky had at least looked at the script. My mouth fell open when I spotted Rhoda Spark—the prepubescent, large-bosomed youngster from the soap audition—also known as Nip Slip. Rhoda had not been at the rehearsals. She was clearly an extra hired for the episode.

She waved like we were long lost friends. I waved back and was delighted and relieved to see none of her privates were openly on display. At the very least, she was a familiar face who was happy to see me. It was also nice to see that she had a job. Granted, extra work didn't pay well, but it was something. Rhoda seemed like a nice kid… with enormous boobs. Ironically, I'd seen her a few times since the fateful day of the soap audition—mostly at Target. And most of the time she hadn't been flashing nip. There was hope for Rhoda yet.

The execs sat in folding chairs along the back wall of the soundstage and were chatting amongst themselves. Several were typing on tablets and a few were on their phones. There would be a new script after the run-through. Notes would be given to the showrunners. Freak outs and yelling fights would ensue. Occasionally, there would be tears from the writer's room. It would be a creative smackdown.

And then... the new and improved script would arrive after lunch, only to be improved again the next day. It only sucked if they were still *improving* five minutes before the final taping. That fell into the category of shitshow.

Avoiding eye contact with the scowling exec was difficult since I could feel his furious gaze on me, but I shook it off. Dealing with Jonny Benji Runky, who looked seriously hung over, was about all I could handle at the moment.

Mean Hot Dude could screw himself. I wasn't getting paid enough to kiss ass.

"And ACTION!" the director yelled.

In exactly five seconds flat, it was painfully clear that Jonny Benji Runky had *not* read the script. I'd bet good money he didn't even know the name of the show. He reeked of alcohol. The rest of the cast wore expressions reminiscent of deer caught in headlights. They were lucky. They didn't have lines with the inebriated ass.

I did.

"So, Ted," I said, reciting my lines to Jonny Benji Runky. "Looks like the shipment of cheese is going to be late. What the heck are we going to do? With the Feta Festival coming up tomorrow we're in a real pickle."

Several of the execs chuckled. It took all I had not to roll my eyes. The dialogue was bad.

Jonny Benji Runky looked confused. "Who the fuck is Ted?"

"Umm... you are," I told him with the friendliest smile I could muster up given the circumstances.

"Right," he slurred. "My bad. Say the line again."

Not one to make a scene, I followed the direction from the jerk. "So, Ted, looks like the shipment of cheese is going to be late. What the heck are we going to do? With the Feta Festival coming up tomorrow we're in a real pickle."

Jonny Benji Runky belched. "Not my problem."

I glanced over at the director in alarm. He just shrugged and signaled for me to keep going. Thankfully, I had a memory like a steel trap and knew Jonny Benji Runky's lines almost as well as my own.

"Maybe we can bring the town together for an overnight cheese-making party! It would be an awesome bonding experience and Old Farmer Gene McBunkel can play the fiddle and clog!"

"It's McGunkle," the script supervisor corrected me.

I closed my eyes and pressed the bridge of my nose. I wanted to headbutt her, but didn't see that as a good option. "Umm… yep. Sorry about that. It wasn't actually my line."

Jonny Benji Runky went from confused to bewildered. "Whose line was it?"

"Yours," I replied as the entire cast and crew paled to the point I thought there might be a mass pass out. Only Rhoda Spark gave me a thumbs up—not necessarily a good omen. Unfortunately, I heard a few gasps from the execs. The director was sweating profusely. None of these things were working in my favor. Well… except Rhoda. However, I was quite sure her opinion didn't count.

Jonny Benji Runky was about to throw a tantrum.

I was very aware that I was in the right and Jonny-boy was in the wrong in this vomit-inducing situation, but fair wasn't a word often used in the business of show. This was ridiculous. However, it wasn't over yet.

"Hey, you," Jonny Benji Runky shouted, pointing at me.

"Me?"

"Yeah, you," he snapped with an ugly sneer. "Who do you think you are?"

"I'm Cec—" I started, only to be cut off.

"I don't care who you are," he bellowed. "You're a nobody. Turn around and show them your ass."

"I'm sorry, what?" I choked out. I felt the blood rush to my face and the need to punch Jonny Benji Runky in his junk consumed me. Assaulting the star of the show would land me in the tabloids—a place I didn't want to be. The choices were poor, but a lawsuit as opposed to turning around was preferable. It felt as if I was having an out-of-body experience.

Sadly, I was still in my body.

Swallowing every bit of pride I owned, I did as directed. It was sexist and probably illegal, but calling Man-mom for bail after I'd punched Jonny Benji Runky in the testicles wasn't the best plan. I died a thousand little deaths as I turned my back on the cast, crew and network execs to display my rear end.

"Look at her ass," Jonny Benji Runky shouted. "It's not bootylicious. While I'd definitely tap that hot ass, it's not the ass I requested. What the fuck is going on here? I can't work like this. I've been nominated for two People's Choice Awards in case any of you assholes might have forgotten. This is MY SHOW. Get me a big juicy ass—a huge fucking ass—or I quit."

On that lovely note, Jonny Benji Runky threw his unread script at the wall of the cheese shop and stomped off the set.

My ass was still facing the crowd.

The silence was deafening.

I couldn't have turned around for world peace.

I was so furious with myself for not walking off the set when I was told to show my ass, I was shaking. In the era of Me Too, this was bullshit.

The stage manager cleared his throat—six times. "Let's take lunch. Everyone back on set in an hour."

I looked at no one. I thought I heard Jenni call my name, but I was so close to humiliated sobbing, I didn't stop. Running from the soundstage, I sprinted all the way to my truck. What the hell was I thinking? This wasn't the life or career I wanted. It was degrading, and not one asshole exec had stood up for me. However, I was more pissed at myself than anyone else. I hadn't stood up for myself either.

It was all about the money. People like me were dispensable. Jonny Benji Runky made big bucks for the network. His shitty behavior came with the territory. A blind eye was always turned when dollars were involved.

That kind of behavior was unacceptable in my book.

Thankfully, my phone was in the pocket of the heinous suit I was still wearing. Letting my head fall to the steering wheel, I waited for the call. I'd been around too long not to recognize the writing on the wall.

∽

"BABY! CECILY!" BEYONCE YELLED INTO THE PHONE.

I yanked it away from my ear and dropped it onto the passenger seat. My agent was so loud, I didn't even need to put her on speakerphone.

It had taken a good half hour before the call I'd predicted was coming actually came. I'd had time to cry, fix my makeup then meditate. I regretted not pocketing one of Sean's gummies. I could have used some jazz cabbage to dull my ugly reality.

"Hey, Beyonce," I said, forcing my lips into a smile so I sounded semi-normal.

"Legally going by Britney now," she informed me. "I got some good news and some bad news. What do you want first?"

"I got fired. Right?" I asked, before she could say it.

"Yes, and it's not your fault, baby," she said. "From what I could make out, your ass didn't have the right feel for the show."

I started laughing. I was pretty sure she thought I was crying.

"Personally, I think that's bullshit. I'd kill for your ass," Britney told me. "They said while there was nothing specifically wrong with your ass, it's not the ass they were looking for. They're going to move on and find a more appropriate ass."

"They're all asses," I said, picking up the phone and speaking into it so she could hear me.

"Agreed," she bellowed.

I gave up and put her on speakerphone. I didn't need hearing loss on top of an already horrible day.

"Here's the bottom line," Britney went on. "You're getting paid for all eight episodes. I also threatened to sue for harassment after one of my clients texted and let me know what the sloshed comedian son of a bitch actually said to you."

"Oh my God," I choked out on a laugh. "You threatened to sue?"

"You bet your very nice and appropriately-sized ass I did," she shouted with glee. "Those suits choked on their own spit I tell you! It was a beautiful moment. I recorded the entire conversation to use in court."

"Is that legal?" I asked with a wince. There was no way I was going to court. I didn't need that kind of publicity. Hell, I was ready to call it quits on the entire business. The magic was very close to disappearing.

"Probably not legal," Britney admitted with a sad sigh. "But the rags will love it."

"Nope," I said quickly. "I just want this over. Pretty sure I'm done."

There was silence on the other end of the line.

"Done, done?" Britney asked in a choked whisper.

I sighed and replayed the mortifying five minutes on the set in my mind. If something like that ever happened again, it was going to play out very differently. No way in hell was I going to keep my mouth shut. However, if I took myself out of the rat race there was no possibility of it happening again.

"I think so," I told her truthfully.

"Do you hate me?" she asked.

"Umm... no," I replied. A small grin tugged at my lips.

Beyonce-Gaga-Madonna-Britney's game was always the same. She rarely veered from the script. Since my memory was outstanding, I knew every line that was about to be thrown my way.

"You do," Britney lamented. "You hate me with the fire of a thousand blazing suns."

"Nope. Five hundred suns," I corrected her.

"Not funny!" she shouted with a cackle of laughter. "I get absurd, almost orgasmic pleasure out of repping you, Cecily."

"TMI," I said.

"It's true," she insisted. "*Camp Bite* was my favorite show. Saved my damn life. Got me through a nasty divorce with husband number three. Watching you and your brother outsmart werewolves and go head-to-head with aliens kept me sane. The disco contest with the witches and wizards was genius."

I would not have gone that far. Quick-thinking and dorky, maybe. Genius? Absolutely not.

"Seriously, I know the Oscar-worthy talent you have inside you," Britney said. "No one has seen what I see… yet."

Her words made me feel happy and sad. I felt the same way. If I ever got my hands on the right material, there would be no stopping me unless I chose to stop myself. But the truth was, I was getting tired. It had been a long road and the pot of golden dreams at the end of the rainbow seemed so far away.

"Oh! I left out the important good news," Britney said, conveniently ignoring the part of the conversation about me getting out of the business.

My hands were on the steering wheel. My knuckles were white from the grip. If I let Britney talk, I knew I'd be tempted. All I'd ever wanted to do my entire life was act—to be someone I wasn't. If I was being honest… and why not? Acting made me whole. I was the motherless child who had always hoped that somewhere, somehow, the woman who didn't want me was watching me on TV or in the movies… and that she was proud. Or at least regretted abandoning me.

My therapist had a field day with that one. She'd suggested that I was trying to change myself into someone who my absent mother would love—that I believed I wasn't enough. Our work together was to get me to believe that I *was* enough.

At forty, I wasn't sure I was there yet.

But I was trying. And I did love acting. Screw my mother. It was for me.

"Okay," I said slowly. "What's the good news?"

I could literally feel Britney vibrating with excitement on the other end of the call. "In order to avoid a lawsuit, I negotiated a little deal for you… and ultimately me, since I get fifteen percent."

I laughed. You couldn't say my agent wasn't honest. "And that deal would be?"

"Ready for it?" Britney squealed.

"Nope."

"Great! You have a deal for your own sitcom. Twenty-two episodes guaranteed. Pay or play. And at your quote!" she belted out. "I'm a producer on the mother humper and you have full creative license. You pick the showrunners, cast, crew, the whole shebang! We have to deal with only one network exec. I'm a freaking GODDESS!"

Now I almost choked on my own spit. "Are you serious?"

"No! I'm Britney, bitch." She laughed. "But about the deal? Hell to the yes! You're the boss, baby. And it's about time."

"Which exec?" I asked.

"Didn't recognize the name. Someone new."

I shook my head to clear it. This was nuts. Had my utter humiliation turned into a win? The way it was gotten was shady, but I wasn't. I was good at what I did. Maybe I could finally show the rest of the world what I could do.

Was this going to blow up in my face?

Not a clue. It remained to be seen.

CHAPTER FOUR

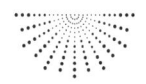

"It can't be right—too good to be true," I said to my dashboard, still absorbing the bomb Britney had dropped.

My agent had assured me at least ten times that she wasn't pulling my leg before we'd hung up. The insane woman had also informed me she was calling her lawyer to get her name changed from Britney to Mariah. It was getting impossible to keep up. She'd told me to go to Gucci and buy a bag to celebrate. That wasn't my thing. Due to my upbringing, I was more of an outlet kind of gal and Target made me salivate. I didn't care how much money I had, I didn't like to waste it on trendy stuff.

Although, I did have a shoe fetish. I'd been eyeing a sequined pair of Doc Martens for three months. Maybe I'd splurge. Even if the deal Britney, soon to be Mariah, had sworn up and down she'd gotten was accurate, it didn't mean it would definitely happen. It might fall through. It wasn't my first time at the dog and pony show. However, I knew I'd be paid for the eight episodes of *Family Spies* I wasn't doing. That was fairly standard.

Glancing down, I groaned in disgust.

"Jesus," I muttered, wincing at the heinous eggplant suit I was wearing—or at this juncture, had stolen.

There was no way I was stepping foot into the studio to return the ugly costume and get my clothes back.

"Damn, my favorite jeans are in there… Wait. Jenni can help me," I said aloud. Talking to myself was my normal MO. "Text Jenni. She'll snag my jeans. That's what friends are for… to grab your clothes after you showed your ass to thirty people."

Grabbing my phone, I pulled up her contact info.

Jenni, can u get my jeans? They're in dressing room E. No way I can come back in. I texted.

She texted right back. *You got it. P.S. All hell has broken lose in here.*

More specific. I sent back.

Jonny Benji Runky just got his ass handed to him—pun intended.

As in fired? My fingers flew over the keyboard with glee.

Nope. As in a black eye, split lip and a possibly dislocated shoulder. She texted back with ten laughing emojis.

I stared at the text with my mouth open. Karma didn't usually work so fast. *Shut the front door. Details please.*

There was a two-minute lag while I waited for a reply. *Tomorrow. Lunch. Noon. Mexican by the studio lot. Have to mop up blood. It was poetic.*

It's a date. See u then.

Roger that. I'll get your things and we'll tie one on tomorrow.

I laughed. *Looking forward to it. Love u.*

Love u more.

I stared at my phone. My grin was wide. I was sure I'd read about the smackdown in the rags tomorrow. Normally, I avoided the tabloids at all cost, but today had not been normal.

Crossing my fingers, I hoped my non-bootylicious butt wasn't part of the gossip.

Removing the ugly jacket and tossing it to the backseat, I reached over to the passenger-side floor and grabbed the extra set of workout clothes I kept handy. Thank God, I was an anally organized person. Driving home naked was preferable to wearing the offensive business suit for another second. Thankfully, I didn't have to. I had sweatpants, a t-shirt and running shoes in the truck.

Shimmying out of the tight skirt was difficult but doable. I was on a mission to obliterate anything that had to do with *Family Spies*.

"I'm winning," I sang as I expertly navigated avoiding a hip bruise from bashing into the steering wheel while I pulled on my sweats.

Literally tearing off the starched ruffled blouse, I laughed as the buttons popped off and scattered all over. Life was going to be okay. Jonny Benji Runky had gotten kicked in the balls by the Universe and I was going to create my own show.

"Unreal and freaking awesome," I muttered as I adjusted my bra straps that had loosened under the nasty blouse.

Things were looking up. I smiled at my reflection in the rearview mirror and gave myself a cheesy thumbs up.

Then I screamed.

I screamed at the top of my lungs.

I screamed like I was auditioning for a horror movie and my mortgage depended on it.

I screamed so loud I was pretty sure I'd ruptured my larynx.

The tap on the driver's-side window was unexpected. The fact that I was only wearing a bra and sweats was mortifying. The person on the other side of the window was wildly unwelcome. His glare was even more terrifying up close.

Quickly pulling the t-shirt over my head since the asshole was staring at my girls, I took a deep breath to compose myself. I also grabbed the mace from the glove compartment. I wasn't playing games.

"Who are you and what do you want?" I croaked out rudely, rolling down the window. My throat was on fire and I sounded like I was whispering.

"You and I need to have a chat," the beautiful, pissed-off man ground out.

I squinted at him and aimed the mace at his eyes. "I don't know you. I'm not chatting with someone who clearly doesn't like me."

The man ran his hand through his hair and muttered something to himself that I missed. I didn't miss the next part.

"*Doesn't like* isn't accurate," he said smoothly.

His voice was freaking hypnotic. His words were not.

"*Can't stand* would be more accurate," he clarified.

I maced him.

It felt great. I was shocked I'd done it. However, it didn't affect him at all. I scanned the can for an expiration date. Couldn't find one. Shit.

"As I was saying before you tried to blind me," he went on as if what had just occurred was nothing out of the ordinary, "we need to talk."

"Nope," I said, grabbing my phone, ready to call 911.

"You have no choice, Cecily. You're in danger."

"Understatement," I muttered under my breath.

The area wasn't deserted. It was broad daylight. There were a few people milling around the parking lot. It was lunchtime. If he attacked, there would be witnesses. However, if the hot mean dude was carrying a gun with a silencer, no one would even know I was dead until security walked the parking lot later this evening.

"I'm calling the cops," I snapped, still having volume issues due to my screaming episode.

"Good luck," he replied, leaning on the car parked next to mine.

My phone was dead. What the heck? It was fully charged five minutes ago.

"I am so out of here," I muttered, pressing the button to start my truck.

It was dead too.

No phone. No truck. No voice to call for help and the mace was useless.

Talk about being screwed... I never should have left the house today. Now, I really regretted not eating the bagel and the donuts.

I might be about to bite it. Fine. At the very least I'd get a name and jot it down so when my mutilated body was found, my dad and brother would have something to go on. It was very clear to me that I watched too many crime dramas on TV. From now on, I'd watch comedies only... if I was still alive ten minutes from now.

"Speak, asshole," I said. "Name first."

"My name is Abaddon," he replied. "My friends call me Abe. You can call me Abaddon."

"I'll stick with *Dick*," I shot back, rolling my eyes. If he was going to snap my neck I could be as rude as I wanted. "Say what you have to say, Dick. I have places to be and things to do."

He shrugged and glanced around. The move terrified me. Was he checking for witnesses if he offed me? Again, did I watch too much TV?

Probably and probably.

"This conversation should take place somewhere more private," he suggested.

"Not happening."

He was close enough to the truck that if I opened the door really fast and with force, I could possibly make him fall. I could get out and run. I was a fast runner. There was no way he could get away with my murder if I could get back into the studio.

"Don't try it," Abaddon, *Abe to his friends*, said with an annoyed expression on his stupidly handsome face.

I inhaled deeply, grabbed a notebook from the passenger seat and wrote my goodbye letter to my dad and brother. I made sure to include the name and description of my killer. He would probably destroy the evidence after the deed was done, but at least I'd tried.

"I'm ready now," I stated. "Spit out whatever you want to say then make my murder quick. I'd prefer painless too if you can manage that, Dick."

He rolled his eyes. "If only," he muttered. "Unfortunately, I'm not here to kill you. I'm here to protect you."

I laughed. The man might be pretty but he was a tremendously bad liar.

"Awesome. I've always wanted a bodyguard named Dick who hated my guts."

"I don't have time for this shit," he said, shaking his head. "So, I'll just lay it out since you're averse to chatting someplace private. I'd planned on easing you into it, but you're a fucking nightmare."

"Thank you. So are you. I'm all ears, Dick," I replied, lifting my middle finger and giving him a smile that came nowhere near reaching my eyes.

He laughed. It was breathtaking. I shook my head to get rid of my wildly inappropriate thoughts. It was far too early in our nonexistent relationship for me to be having Stockholm Syndrome.

"You're not normal," he informed me.

I rolled my eyes. "Who is? If you want to insult me, you lost. No one in LA is normal."

"You're a Demon," he said with a straight face.

"Been called worse," I told him. "You have anything else?"

His brows shot up and he scowled. "I'm serious."

"No, you're not Serious," I explained to him in the voice I would use with a child. "You're Dick. And I think you could use a good therapist."

"Pain in my ass," he said, scrubbing his hand over his jaw. "If I prove it to you, will you believe me?"

"Probably not, but go for it, Dick."

His lips compressed to a thin angry line. Pretty sure he didn't like being called Dick. Too bad, so sad.

My murderer removed a contact from each of his eyes. I almost swallowed my tongue. Dick had the very same eyes that I did—Goat Eyes. Where his pupils should have been were shimmering silver horizontal lines instead.

"Demon," he said flatly, pointing to his eyes.

I removed the contact from my left eye. "Birth defect," I shot back. "You're gonna have to do better than that, Dickie-boy."

Glancing around again, he leaned in closer. "Would you like to go to Hell?"

I laughed. "If that's how you ask a girl out, you need some new lines. And again, I'm recommending therapy, *Dick*."

"Done," he snapped. "I don't get paid enough to deal with this."

He waved his hands. I felt a blast of heat surge through my veins. This was going to be a shitty way to die. Dick had clearly ignored my request for a pain-free demise.

My head pounded and my skin felt like it was melting off my body. I couldn't see a thing. Screaming was useless. The roar in my ears was so loud I could barely think. An arid wind whipped through my hair and the sensation of falling into an abyss consumed me.

It seemed to go on for eternity.

And then it stopped.

"Open your eyes, Cecily," Dick instructed in a curt tone.

"I'm dead. I can't."

"You're not dead yet," he countered. "Open your eyes, take a peek at your heritage."

Slowly, I opened my eyes.

If this was my heritage, I wanted to trade it in for something a little less inferno-like.

A vast mountainous landscape of raging fire lay in front of me as far as my eyes could see. The words wicked and sultry came to mind as I watched the flames lick up the sides of trees bearing fruit I'd never seen. Swarms of brightly colored birds soared through the fire. Their wing spans were the size of a car and the sounds they made reminded me of metal on metal in a deadly pileup of cars. My breath came in quick spurts and I felt a strange kinship to the shocking scene. A huge red sun hung low in an inky purple sky. I glanced down to see what I was standing on, and gasped.

Nothing.

I was standing on air next to the meanest guy named Dick I'd ever come across. I was pretty sure he'd drugged me and this was a seriously messed-up hallucination. Or maybe he'd knocked me out and taken me to a special-effects-pyrotechnics show. However, the searing heat kind of made that unlikely.

"Get me out of here," I hissed as my desire to stay increased.

Dick had slipped me some heavy-duty drugs.

"Take it in," he said emotionlessly. "It's probably the only time you'll ever witness it."

"Fine by me," I snapped.

He glanced over at me. His beauty was absurd and he fit right into the furious fiery hallucination he'd caused. I wasn't exactly sure how he was here with me and we were talking, but making sense of an acid trip wasn't my forte. I'd have to talk to Sean about it later if I was actually still alive.

"Close your eyes, Cecily," Dick ordered.

I rolled my eyes first and then did as requested. Looking at Dick wasn't smart. He was clearly evil but very pretty. I kept picturing things I shouldn't—naked things. The fact that he hated me was good.

God, I had shitty taste in men.

"Relax," my drug dealer said, taking my hand in his. "It's easier to travel if you let yourself go."

Was he talking about death or leaving the drug-induced fire pit? Did it matter? No. There didn't seem to be much of a choice.

Again, I felt like Alice falling through the looking glass. The inferno I'd just seen was now inside me. The sensation of wanting to peel my skin off was strong. My teeth ached and my hair hurt like it had been in a tight ponytail for a week. I reached out for something to grasp as I continued to fall.

With a cry of relief, I grabbed the steering wheel of my truck.

Wait. What?

"What the fu...?" I muttered, checking myself to make sure I hadn't been burned alive. My skin felt flushed and my head still spun a bit. I was back in my pickup… or back from my acid trip. Right now, it was a fifty-fifty toss-up.

"Was that sufficient?" Dick inquired.

"You mean did you give me enough LSD?" I shot back sarcastically.

Dick the wannabe Demon drug dealer who needed a shrink blew out a long, slow breath. Sadly, it was sexy. He pulled a card out of his pocket and put it on the dash of my car.

"You're a Demon. I'm a Demon," he said flatly. "There are other Demons who want you dead."

"If you say so." I picked up his card and flicked it at him.

His Goat Eyes narrowed dangerously. "Ask your father about it. He knows. If you don't believe me, you might believe the man who raised you."

"Let's make a deal," I said, turning the ignition on my truck and almost crying with joy that it started.

His fists clenched at his sides. Dick was a dick. "Your terms?"

"I'll talk to my dad and you call a shrink," I suggested, giving him one last middle finger salute.

Abaddon—Abe to all but me—returned the favor. I laughed and drove away. The man was certifiable, and I hoped I never saw him again in this lifetime.

CHAPTER FIVE

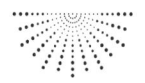

"Eat one of these. They're the mild kind. Nice and easy—barely gets you buzzed," Sean insisted, handing me a jazz cabbage gummy. "Shit's gone haywire."

I accepted it gladly. Haywire didn't quite suffice, but it was close.

Man-mom looked like he'd aged a hundred years. He sat on the sage-green velvet couch in my cozy living room, bent forward and holding his balding head in his hands. His paint-splattered pants and shirt were his normal attire. The setting sun cast a golden glow over the room through the bay window. The comforting beauty was in stark juxtaposition to my mood.

For four and a half hours, my dad had spouted fiction. For the same amount of time, I'd called bullshit. While my job required pretending, real life did not.

During the hours-long stupefying conversation, for lack of a better term, Sean had made sub sandwiches and a pan of brownies. I avoided the brownies. My brother only made jazz cabbage desserts. I needed my wits about me even though my family seemed to have lost theirs. He'd made my sub without bread since I'd sworn off carbs. The lettuce-wrapped salami, ham and cheese came close to making me lose my debatably sane mind. When his head was turned, I swiped his sandwich. My amazing sibling didn't flinch. He happily ate the lettuce wrap and watched with amusement as I inhaled his and made sure I didn't miss a single crumb of bread.

"Abe is correct," Man-mom said quietly. "You're a Demon—well, half Demon."

"Wait. Dick lets you call him *Abe*?" I asked, realizing it was the least important of all the questions swirling like a tornado in my brain.

My dad seemed confused but nodded. "I've only ever known him as Abe."

"Unbelievable," I shouted as I got up and began to search the room. I had no clue why it had taken me four hours to figure out what was going on. But in my defense, it had been a whopper of a day.

My retelling of my firing pissed off both my dad and brother. Jonny Benji Runky's karmic racking made them laugh and high five. The news about getting a sitcom deal made both men cheer. Then I got to the part about my trip to Hell. Sean was sure I was making it up. To be honest, I wondered if he was correct. However, Man-mom paled to the point of ghostly and began to talk… and talk… and talk.

The word *unbelievable* worked for everything my dad confessed. I didn't believe I was a Demon. Demons were fiction just like vampires and werewolves. Not for one second did I buy that my *Demon* mother had left this realm for my own safety when she realized I was also a *Demon*. And I really couldn't believe that Dick let my dad call him Abe.

"I'll find them," I muttered, searching under the furniture and behind the curtains.

Picking up a throw pillow from the overstuffed armchair that I let no one sit on but me, I wanted to rip it to shreds. I knew they were here. I just had to find them. Unsure if Sean was in on the gag, but assuming he might be, I vowed to get both of the men in my life back in a big fat hairy way.

"What are you looking for?" Sean asked, handing me another gummy.

I shook my head no to the Devil's Lettuce mood enhancer. One was enough for me. "Looking for the cameras," I muttered, removing the pictures from the walls and running my hands over the plaster.

"Your place is bugged?" Sean choked out, immediately hiding all of the pot products. "I might be in a little trouble here."

Man-mom sighed and gave me a weak smile. "The house isn't bugged," he assured my brother, who let out such a relieved grunt it would have been funny if I wasn't in such a knot.

"I'm being punked," I said, continuing to scour the living room. "There's no other explanation."

"There is. And if you would sit down and open your mind for a moment we can get to the truth together," my dad said, taking my shaking hand in his and leading me to the couch.

I stared at him.

He stared at me.

He was a beautiful man. He was a good man. He loved me. I knew that as fact.

Maybe he had early-onset dementia.

"I love you, Cecily-boo," he said, gently touching my cheek.

"I love you more," I whispered, placing my hand over his.

He smiled. "Not possible."

Man-mom had flecks of pink paint in his long lashes. My

eyes filled. If he was losing it, I could play along. There was very little I wouldn't do for the person who had raised me and loved me to the moon and back. I made a mental note to take him in for a medical evaluation. If there was some kind of therapy or meds for him, I would be all over it.

"Okay," I said, sitting down on the couch and closing my eyes for a hot second. "Tell me the truth, Dad."

His left brow shot up in surprise. I rarely called him Dad. Usually it was Man-mom with the occasional Bill thrown in for emphasis.

"Never thought we'd have this discussion," he admitted, scratching his head absently. "Your mom said you would never be in danger unless you knew. Not real sure why Abe feels it's right to tell you now. You've been safe for forty years."

I stayed silent. The only words that came to mind were dripping in sarcasm. That wouldn't help my dad's mental state.

"I didn't know Lilith was a Demon when we fell in love," he reminisced fondly. "Most beautiful gal I'd ever seen—inside and out. You look so much like her, Cecily."

I nodded. That much I knew. He'd shared that with me over the years. The fact didn't thrill me since she didn't want me, but it was what it was.

"Found out she wasn't of this world by accident when a few unsavory denizens from Hell ambushed us on a Tuesday Night Date Night. We'd had a lovely Italian supper and decided to walk off the pasta and wine on the beach. Nice starry evening."

Sean was taking notes. I was positive a weird poem was going to be borne of this farked-up heart to heart.

"What happened next?" Sean asked.

I wasn't sure if my brother was buying the yarn my dad was spinning or if he had the same suspicions about Man-mom's mind that I did. It didn't matter. We'd discuss it when we were alone.

"Well, we were attacked by hulking men with Goat Eyes," Dad explained with a rueful smile pulling at his lips. "Huge Demons—completely on fire. Never saw anything like it. At first, I wondered if they were shooting a movie on the beach, but that wasn't the case. The bastards were gunning for us."

"Holy shit," Sean muttered, leaning forward and nibbling on a brownie.

"And then some," Dad agreed with a chuckle. "Tried to push your mom behind me. Didn't think I'd live through it, but I was hoping I could make sure she did."

It was all I could do not to cry. Not about the story. It was absurd. My tears were for how far gone my dad actually was.

He looked at me and smiled. I was pretty sure he knew I didn't believe a word, but he kept going. "Damnedest thing happened next. Your mom snapped her fingers and all of a sudden, she was wielding a sword made of purple fire. In a matter of a minute, Lilith lopped off the heads of the Demons. Those sons of bitches didn't stand a chance."

"Got it," I said, just wanting it to be over. The more he spoke, the more worried I became.

"You don't," he said gently. "But you will. It took a few days of explanations from your mom, but in the end, I realized I didn't care what she was. I loved her with everything I had and she loved me the same. Found out we were pregnant a week later and went on with our wonderful little life until she had to go."

"Question," Sean said, still jotting notes. "Did you love my mom and did she happen to be a Demon as well? Or possibly a werewolf or succubus?"

Man-mom laughed and shook his head. "I did love your

mom. It was a different kind of love than I had with Lilith, but equally as wonderful. And no, she was one hundred percent human."

"Well, that sucks," Sean muttered.

I squinted at him. Was it possible that he believed the crap our dad was spewing? Or was it the pot talking?

"Not at all, Sean," Man-mom said. "Your mom was a free spirit—a true artist. She moved with the wind. I knew she wouldn't stay, but I was blessed to have part of her always." He smiled at his son. "You're the best of both me and your mom. You and your sister are my reason and my light."

The three of us sat in silence and absorbed all the revelations.

Man-mom yawned and stood up. "There are more tales to tell, but I'm bushed. Mind if we continue in the morning? I need to finish up a painting. It's a commission."

I stood and wrapped my arms around my dad. Sean joined the hug and we held each other without a word spoken. After a kiss to each of our foreheads, Man-mom slowly walked back over to his and Sean's abode. Part of my heart broke away and left with him.

"Wow," Sean muttered as he began to clean up the dinner mess. "That was something else."

I picked up a full-sugared soda from the coffee table and downed it. My diet wasn't happening today. Tomorrow was another story… maybe. "You believe him?"

"Yep," Sean confirmed. "Don't you?"

"No. I don't."

Sean stared at me for a long moment then winked. "As Arthur Conan Doyle said, once you eliminate the impossible, whatever remains, no matter how improbable, must be the truth. Oh, and Uncle Joe is back."

"Uncle Joe is dead," I reminded my brother.

"Somebody should let him know. He drew a penis on Man-mom's cockroach."

"Did you see him?" I demanded, rolling my eyes.

"Nope." Sean shook his head.

"Then how do you know that Uncle Joe—*who is dead*—drew the dick on the cockroach?" I couldn't even fathom that I'd just put that sentence together.

"He signed it," Sean informed me. "Wrote, *Dick by Dancing Joe*."

I didn't even have words. Was my entire family losing it? Both my dad and Sean had sworn up and down that Uncle Joe was paying visits. Uncle Joe was six feet under. Therefore, it was not possible. He'd been dead for a year. Joe was my dad's beloved older brother. He was a fabulous nutjob—had lived in a nudist colony for decades and then when he went into the assisted living home, he'd refused to wear clothes. While I did adore Uncle Joe, it was difficult to hang out with him due to his aversion to wearing pants. He enjoyed dancing. Naked. He'd died in a bare-assed attempt at breakdancing—heart attack. Didn't suffer a bit.

Whatever. If we were all losing our minds, we had each other. There was strength in numbers.

My brother's words stayed with me long after he'd gone home to his bungalow next door—not the Uncle Joe part, the Arthur Conan Doyle quote. Maybe I was the one having a mental break and Man-mom and Sean were fine.

Or maybe all of us were batshit crazy.

The Mexican restaurant was colorful, familiar and a place I adored. Waving at a few of the gals and guys who worked at the establishment, I spotted my buddy in the back.

Today was a new day. Yesterday was history and I refused to go backwards. Stories about Demons and cockroaches with penises were best left in the past.

"Look at this," Jenni said gleefully, pushing the rag mag to my side of the table as I sat down in the quiet corner booth she'd chosen for us.

I scanned the front page as I tucked my purse behind me and my mouth fell open. "What the heck? Who made *that* happen?"

The headline read, *Runky Goes To Rehab*. The article went on to say that Jonny Benji Runky wanted the world to know that he had a problem. He admitted he was a sexist jerk who had issues with alcohol. The comedian was proud to let his fans know that he needed help and would be starting a foundation to help other sexists. He went on to talk about all seven of his failed marriages and how embarrassed he was that he couldn't recall three of his ex-wife's names. It was at that very moment that Jonny realized he had a problem. And after physically beating himself up in the dressing room of his hit TV show with a sex toy, he realized he needed professional assistance. *Family Spies* would be on hiatus for six months while Jonny got healthy.

"The studio made *that* happen," Jenni replied, sipping on a margarita. "However, Jonny Benji Runky did do a phone interview. The dumbass actually called himself a sexist jerk. Heard him say it."

"Five points for self-awareness," I muttered.

"True that," Jenni agreed.

I waved to Tony, the adorable waiter who I'd known

forever, and pointed at Jenni's drink. He nodded and winked. Tony was a seventy-five-year-old gem. "How much of that article do you think is true?" I asked, silently thanking God that the part about Jonny going off on my non-bootylicious ass wasn't in the write up.

Jenni shrugged and grinned. "The only part I can vouch for is that the show's on hiatus and that the idiot called himself a sexist jerk. Hiatus sucks because I won't get paid, but that set was freaking toxic. Old Runky Dunk is an alcoholic, sexist asshole, but the show shut down because he deservedly got his ass handed to him and he has to hide out and heal up. Not even makeup can cover the shiner that guy has."

Sitting with Jenni felt normal. Even though our conversation was anything but normal, it beat the heck out of being told I was a Demon and that my absent mom could click her heels and produce purple swords of fire… or something like that. Shoving my worries about my dad—and quite honestly, myself—to the back of my mind took effort, but I was all about the normal today.

"Beat himself up with a *sex toy*," I read aloud, laughing.

Jenni choked mid-sip and joined me. "Not true. Wish it was, but definitely not true."

"So, who wailed on the asshat?" I asked, scanning the menu then pushing it aside. I already knew what I wanted. It had been the same order since I started coming to the restaurant decades ago—a spicy chicken chimichanga with extra hot sauce on the side, no sour cream.

Yes, it had carbs.

No, I didn't care.

"Best-looking man I've ever seen," Jenni said, perusing the menu. "He's the new head of the studio. Apparently, he was at the run-through, saw Jonny Jackoff in action and didn't like what he saw. I heard him tell the hungover idiot if he ever spoke to you or any other woman like that again, he was done. It was hotter than heck. Rumor has it, Mr. Sexy Feminist Dude bought the entire operation. Man's gotta be richer than Midas. Crazy stuff."

My stomach cramped and I felt myself begin to sweat even though I was wearing a summery mini-dress. "A single person bought the studio? Not a corporation?"

"If the gossip is accurate, then yep—a single, very sexy guy bought the whole shebang." Jenni wrinkled her nose in thought. "But I have no clue if he's single-single. I'd say no. He has to be attached or gay. He's too damn good-looking to be real—looks more like he should be in front of the camera than behind a desk—black hair, hot bod, gorgeous blue eyes, Armani suit. Abe something or other. I didn't catch a last name."

Thinking I might puke, I shook my head and felt a headache named Dick coming on. "That would be in the trades," I insisted, grabbing my phone and pulling up the *Hollywood Report*. Searching the words Keystone Studios, I waited to see if it had been sold. "Nothing. The rumors are false." I felt a huge surge of relief. Mariah had just cut a deal for me at Keystone. If Dick was in charge, that was not good.

Dick hated me and the feeling was mutual.

But wait... if he truly ran the operation now, there was no way he would've let a sweet deal like mine go through. I heaved another sigh of relief. Hopefully, Dick was just another random exec. Plus, half the time, there wasn't a shred of truth to gossip. I wasn't quite sure how it got kept out of the rags that he'd smacked down on Jonny Benji Runky, but ultimately, I didn't care.

Dick the wannabe Demon was not my problem.

Tony took our orders and showed us pictures of his newest grandbaby. She looked just like her grandpa—bald and adorable. While I loved chatting with Tony, I was chomping at the bit to tell Jenni my good news... and offer her a job.

"Got your jeans, shirt, flip-flops and backpack," she said, passing a bag over the table once Tony had left. "Was there anything else?"

"There was a pink thong, but don't worry about it," I told her, grateful to have my favorite jeans back. "And thank you."

Jenni grinned. "Were you going commando under that nasty suit yesterday?"

"Hell no," I told her with a laugh. "It was an extra. Wasn't sure what kind of underthings I'd need with my heinous costume."

She pursed her lips. "Didn't see a thong. I can look again if you want me to. I have to pack up my makeup kits and start calling around to see if anyone needs an artist."

"I know of an awesome job," I said, practically bouncing in my seat.

Jenni perked up. "Do tell."

By the end of my story, where I'd barely taken a breath, Jenni was as excited as I was.

"For real?" she asked for the third time.

"Mariah swore she'd made the deal. She sent the memo over this morning. My lawyer read it over and gave it his stamp of approval. Said he couldn't believe the perks. Totally unheard of," I told Jenni. "I haven't signed it yet, but I have an appointment with the top brass and Mariah in two hours."

"You go gurl," Jenni sang, holding up her glass. "To your new adventure!"

"Our," I corrected her. "I want to talk to Sushi too. She's harsh but brilliant."

"Perfect. Love her," Jenni agreed. "Have you come up with a concept yet?"

"Nope," I said, checking my watch. "I have two hours. You wanna brainstorm a pitch with me?"

"You know I do," she said, pulling out a yellow legal pad and a pen from her bag. "How about this?" Her grin was devious. "Former child star… gets out of the business for a while and is making a comeback. You do a down-and-dirty show about the realities of older women navigating the skeevy underbelly of TV."

"Hits kinda close to home," I said as tingles rushed over my skin.

"Yep," Jenni said, waggling her perfectly plucked brows. "Bet you have a lot of stories that would make hilariously brilliant episodes… Miss I-Don't-Have-A-JLo-Ass."

"That would work?" I asked with a slight wince.

"Dude, the main viewing demographic is women our age. Advertisers will chomp at the bit to buy ad time. Audiences freaking loved you on *Camp Bite*! We keep it close enough to your experiences and far away enough from your real life. It's genius!"

She was right. My entire body was one humongous tingle. I had horrifying audition and work stories that I could twist just a little into solid-gold humor. It was probable that the studio would have ideas already in mind. However, unless Mariah was drunk when she'd made the deal, she'd told me the creative license was all mine. It was in black and white in the contract.

"I just don't know what to call it," Jenni said, nibbling on the end of her pen.

The name hit me like a ton of bricks. My grin was so wide it hurt my face. "I've got it."

"Let's hear it," she said with the pen poised over the paper.

"*Ass the World Turns*," I told her then held my breath.

Jenni's scream brought the entire waitstaff to our booth. When they realized we were laughing and not freaking out, they wandered away. They were used to the weirdo actors and artists. A happy scream was far better than a brawl.

"You like?" I asked, giggling.

"I love! I smell an Emmy."

From Jenni's mouth to the Hollywood God's ears.

Ass the World Turns it was.

CHAPTER SIX

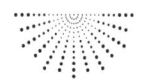

Jenni had insisted on doing my makeup and hair before the big meeting. I'd agreed. She was a magician with her brushes and potions. She'd also heartily approved of the outfit I'd brought to change into. Armed with natural makeup that enhanced what I was born with, a sleek blowout that made my dark shoulder-length hair shine, a super-cool Alice and Olivia dress that I'd gotten on sale and Jimmy Choo slingbacks that I did not get on sale, I felt ready to conquer the world.

"Dude," Jenni said with a grin. "You are one hot forty-year-old mamma who could pass for thirty."

"Been there already," I said with a grin, feeling a little trepidation about being back on the *Family Spies* set, but relieved it was like a ghost town due to the hiatus. "Not going back. I like forty so far."

Jenni had been right about my pretty pink thong. I'd peeked into my former dressing room and it was nowhere to be found. Whatever. I had plenty of flossy string to ride up my rear end. Sean wasn't partial to pilfering my thongs… thank God.

"Amen to loving the life we're living, sis-tah! Go get 'em."

That was my plan.

~

MARIAH AND I WERE THE FIRST TO ARRIVE. THAT WAS TYPICAL. Studio honchos enjoyed keeping the *lesser mortals* waiting. It was part of the game. However, we weren't waiting in the lobby as per the norm. The moment we'd stepped out of the mahogany-paneled elevator, we'd been shown right to an office where the meeting was to be held.

"Jesus," Mariah muttered, looking around with a huge grin on her face.

"And then some," I added, feeling excited and nervous.

It felt like I was teetering on the edge of a cliff that would determine the rest of my career. The sensation was exhilarating and filled with the magic I'd been searching for my entire life. In the scheme of everything, did a sitcom really matter? Technically, no. But art is what we turned to when we wanted to feel alive—whether it be a painting, a book, a movie or even a sitcom. Picasso said, "The purpose of art is washing the dust of daily life off our souls."

The sage words had been the mantra of my acting coach. She'd also said art was art, no matter the medium. Being a tiny part of the magical machine that gave the gift of disappearing into fantasy for however brief a time made me feel whole. Was *Camp Bite* profound? No, absolutely not. Would *Ass the World Turns* bring about world peace? Nope. But it would make people laugh and forget their troubles for a bit. And in the process, I would get to feed my soul with what I felt passion for.

Win-win.

"My office is less than a quarter of the size of this one," Mariah commented, walking around and checking it out.

"I don't even have an office," I added taking in the formality with a strained laugh.

The room was huge and imposing. Someone was clearly compensating for something. I'd never been in this particular building on the lot. It was fairly new and wasn't around during *Camp Bite*. Money oozed from every pore of the over-the-top office. The couches were a buttery brown leather. The walls were a deep shade of green and tasteful art hung on three of them. The fourth wall was floor-to-ceiling windows that had an excellent view of the Hollywood Sign. Hardwood floors, so shiny they looked wet, were partially covered with gorgeous rugs in muted shades of cream and brown. The furniture was heavy and ornate. Everything except the walls was either black, brown or beige. I felt small and inconsequential in the room, which was probably the point.

"Is there lipstick on my teeth?" Mariah asked, showing me her very white and obviously bleached chompers.

Shockingly there wasn't. However, she was sporting a copious amount of lipliner. Mariah loved to line her enhanced lips. "Nope, you look great," I assured her.

She did. She was a tiny little thing with bottle-blonde hair, a well-done boob job, a not-as-well-done nose job and a new set of lips. Her clothes were just a tad too tight and her heels were sky high, but she was gorgeous to me. The mold had been broken sixty-five years ago when Mariah/Britney/Beyonce/Madonna/Gaga was born. I adored her. She'd believed in me when I wasn't sure I believed in myself. She was a total keeper, lipliner and all.

"This is just a formality," Mariah reminded me as she walked behind the massive desk and began snooping through the drawers. "We're just here to put our John Hancocks on the contract."

"Can I make a suggestion?" I inquired with a wince as she picked up what looked like a solid gold plaque and examined her reflection.

"You bet, my favorite client that I've ever had in my whole damn life."

I rolled my eyes. I was pretty sure she used the same line with all of her clients. "Why don't you come out from behind the desk so we don't get busted for spying on the brass."

Mariah laughed and gave me a thumbs up. "Good thinking," she replied. "Habit from childhood. Used to open all my Christmas presents early and rewrap them as a kid. Didn't find out until I was an adult that my mom knew. She got a real kick when I would scream, cry and pretend to be surprised Christmas morning. I was a character even back then."

I laughed. Character was an understatement. Mental note… hide everything incriminating when Mariah comes to dinner.

"So, the meeting's with the exec who we'll be working with on the show?" I asked, bodily removing her from behind the desk and steering her over to the couch.

"Bingo, baby," she confirmed. "Got a message an hour ago that they want to start production ASAP. Apparently, *Family Spies* went on hiatus because that idiot comedian beat himself up with a sex toy and they had to shut down production. Keystone has a hole in the schedule and they want to plug it with your show."

"Umm… very little of that makes sense," I said with a sinking feeling. "We don't even have an actual show yet. It's not like we can go into production tomorrow."

"Not a problem," Mariah said. "I came up with the concept. I have a potential cast list, director list, crew list, writing staff and designer options. Ain't nobody gonna put Mariah in a corner."

I was stunned and somewhat terrified. While my agent was a ball-buster and an incredible negotiator, her taste left a little to be desired—so did her movie references. "You did that in an hour?" I asked.

"Hell to the no," she bellowed with a laugh that sounded like a car horn. "Haven't slept since the offer came in. I'm running on caffeine, adrenaline and a truckload of concealer right now. We're not gonna miss a beat here, baby. I got you the best offer I've ever heard of in my entire career. I'm taking no chances."

She had a point. Even my lawyer had been gobsmacked by the terms. I knew Mariah could compile an outstanding list of amazing behind-the-scenes people. She was savvy and smart in that department. It was the show concept that was potentially horrifying. "Tell me your concept."

"Picture this," she said, getting so excited that she whipped out a makeup pencil and began to line her already overly lined lips without a mirror. "A reboot of *Camp Bites*! But instead of you being the vampire child who solves the crimes, you're all grown up now and running the whole shebang. We have a ritzy summer camp filled with little werewolves and mermaids. Crazy shenanigans ensue! I figure Sean can pop in for some cameos and maybe even Brad Pitt can reprise his role from *Interviews with a Vampire*. Ratings would be insane!"

I was shocked to silence. It was godawful. I couldn't even find my voice to tell her she was using a navy-blue eye pencil to outline her lips. She looked diseased.

Mariah mistook my muteness for I don't even know what. She just kept talking.

"We give you a genie love interest. He lives in a bottle in

your office at the campsite and pops out all the time. His catchphrase is, 'Holy three wishes! What would Barbara Eden do?' I'm telling you, it's pure comedy genius. He'll call you Master. It'll give the show a real *Fifty Shades of Gray* feeling except it'll be family friendly."

Finding my voice was difficult, but imperative. There was no way in hell I wanted her to share this potential disaster with anyone—especially the studio. God forbid anyone else thought it was a good idea.

"Nope," I choked out, getting panicked. "I have a different concept."

"Lemme hear it," Mariah said, still lining her lips in dark blue.

I told her what Jenni and I had come up with. She screamed and practically ate the eye pencil. "That's BRILLIANT!"

My relief was visceral. I insisted that I pitch the concept and she could supply the crew list to the studio. My agent was one hundred percent down with the plan. Right as I was about to point out that her lips were rimmed in navy, the door of the office opened.

All my nightmares came true.

Dick was the exec in charge of my show.

"Ladies," he said as he strolled casually across the office and seated himself behind the desk. "Thank you for coming in."

I realized I was staring daggers at the man who held my professional future in his hands, but I couldn't help myself. Something was very wrong with the picture. I just couldn't put my finger on it yet.

Mariah was practically hyperventilating next to me on the couch. It was all I could do not to shake her silly. Yes, Dick was hotter than sin, but he was a dick. Having my agent react like a rabid teenage fangirl wasn't going to help matters.

"You?" I asked rudely as Mariah looked at me like I'd lost my mind. "You cut this deal? I have to work with *you*?"

His grin was positively feral. If I was being honest—which was totally overrated—I'd have to admit that it did things to my girlie bits. But since it was already established that I had shitty taste in men, I didn't let my reaction throw me. While the attraction might be there, the reality of a one-night stand—much less a relationship—would happen when Hell froze over. The ass had drugged me yesterday, for the love of everything illegal and life threatening.

"That's right," he said smoothly.

Mariah's giggle was so shrill, I almost slapped my hands over my ears. She'd adjusted the neckline of her size six dress that should have been a size eight to reveal more of her sixty-five-year-old silicone cleavage. I closed my eyes and wanted to disappear.

"We're ready to go!" Mariah announced with a shimmy that was appallingly inappropriate. "We've got the concept and all the rest of the jazz, Mr. ummmm…"

"Excellent," Dick said, staring straight at me then turning his intense gaze on the blubbering idiot sitting next to me. "Please call me, Abe—all my friends do."

"Abe," Mariah gushed, blushing. "Call me Mariah."

He nodded curtly then pulled a folder from his drawer. "If both of you could sign on the dotted line, we can get the show started."

"Not how it normally works," I said coolly as Mariah elbowed me to zip my lips.

"This isn't a normal situation," Dick replied just as coolly. "We're in a crunch. We'll start production next week."

My lips compressed. The timeline was insane. Did he want me to fail?

My eyes narrowed and I glared at him. "A successful show takes time and care. I don't want to throw a piece of shit out into the Universe."

"Then don't," he replied with a shrug.

Mariah was about to pass out due to the unfriendly and potentially deal-ending turn of events. Dick pulled a paper bag from a drawer, got up, crossed the room and handed it to her. My agent took it and used it.

Patting Mariah on the back to assure her I could handle the situation, I took a deep breath. "You want me to go into production on Monday? It's Wednesday right now."

"Correct," he said with an obnoxious expression of challenge in his eyes that he'd covered back up with contacts.

Apparently, Goat Eyes weren't appropriate for the office.

I had several choices here. One, tell him to screw himself and walk away from a sure-fire humiliating flop. Two, tell him yes and end up in a humiliating flop. Three, say yes and prove the bastard wrong… if that was possible. All of the choices were bad.

"Fine," I ground out through clenched teeth as Mariah kept panting into the bag. "I'll need an office on the lot and a list of your best available in-house people."

"That can be arranged," he replied.

I wasn't going to be sleeping for the foreseeable future. It was a damn good thing that Jenni was a makeup wizard. I was going to look haggard by the time we shot. That is, if I was still able to keep my eyes open by then.

"I need the show budget, a line producer and some finance people," I reeled off. "A casting director and offices for the writing and production staff. I have people in mind. Need to know how high we can go on salary considering I'll be asking for them to give up their lives."

Dick's expression was difficult to read. I couldn't tell if he was bored or impressed. Didn't matter. I had no plans to fail and I was going to get him to agree to everything I wanted.

"No budget limitations," he replied.

I rolled my eyes. Mariah screamed like she was at the tail end of an orgasm. It was horrifying.

"Bullshit," I said, shaking my head. "What game are you playing?"

"No game," Dick said coldly. "We just lost our top-rated show. We're slightly fucked at the moment."

"Because of you," I pointed out, as Mariah glanced over at me in confusion.

"Wait," she said, still gripping the paper bag like it was a lifeline she might need to use again. "Did Abe supply Jonny Benji Runky with the sex toys that he beat himself up with?"

"Something like that," Dick said with an amused smirk. "Suffice it to say, I need a show and I need it fast. I'm willing to fill the hole with reruns for three to four weeks, and then I expect new product."

"You're insane," I snapped as Mariah began huffing into the paper bag.

"Your point?" he countered.

I'd already made my point. Producing something amazing took time. However, if he was true to his words and gave me three to four weeks, I could make it happen. Maybe.

"Four weeks, not three," I bargained.

He shrugged. "Fine. Four weeks."

"How many episodes?" I asked, sitting on my hands so I didn't flip him off.

"The pilot and one episode ready to go in a month. From there you can continue shooting and keep at least one week ahead of the game. We'll keep production going through the holidays and get ahead for the winter and spring seasons. It's a twenty-two episode deal. Non-negotiable."

"And if it sucks?" I questioned.

Mariah began to dry heave.

"Make sure that doesn't happen," he said.

The silent stare down lasted well over the definition of a socially polite exchange. I wanted to punch Dick in the head. That wasn't professional. I might be an emotional gal, but I was and had always been a pro.

"This is going to cost you a fortune," I said, breaking the hostile silence.

He shrugged. "You get what you pay for."

He was going to be paying through the nose and then some. "I'll sign."

Dick pulled a Montblanc pen from the breast pocket of his expensive suit and held it out. I crossed the room and prayed I didn't attack him by accident. My reaction to him was from the gut and unexplainable. It was also unnerving and made me feel out of control. Mariah crawled across the office on her knees to sign on the dotted line. The harsh exchange had clearly made her lose the ability to walk, let alone breathe.

I signed.

Mariah signed.

Dick signed.

I helped my agent to her feet and turned to leave.

"Mariah, thank you for coming," Dick announced in a brook-no-bullshit tone. "You're free to meet with my assistant and get the ball rolling as far as office space needed and sending out technical offers. Cecily, you will stay. I want to talk concept with you."

"Works for me," Mariah said, pulling herself together and

hugging me so hard I thought the tiny woman might fracture my ribs. "On it!"

She hightailed it out of the office. I was alone with my drug dealer.

Awesome.

"Have a seat, Cecily. We have some unfinished business."

"Will do, Dick," I replied, taking great pleasure as he winced at my pet name for him. "I'm all ears. Tell me more about your Demon fantasy."

He grinned. It freaked me out. "You believe me?"

"Not in a million years, asshole."

He shook his head and chuckled. "You will soon enough."

I rolled my eyes and sat back down on the couch. "Give it your best shot. And good luck."

"I don't need luck," he replied with a smile that would have made my panties melt if I didn't hate the man so much. "I'm that good."

I shrugged and flipped him off. It felt very natural and right to show him my middle finger. "Remains to be seen."

CHAPTER SEVEN

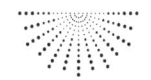

I explained the show. Even though the circumstances were hostile, I found myself getting excited about what the potential of the sitcom could truly be. As funny as I imagined it, I also saw it as an empowering statement for women in their midlife. For a brief moment, I was able to forget that Dick was an insane killer who needed a straightjacket. I let the magic of the project and the possibilities drive me. As I spoke, more ideas came and my passion couldn't be suppressed. The pilot episode I'd pulled out of my butt was a hilarious spin on the horrifying callback from *The Ocean is Deeply Moving*.

Dick's expression was bland and he didn't take a single note in the hour I waxed poetic about *Ass the World Turns*.

I held my breath for a long beat when I finished my pitch. "Thoughts?" I asked.

"Sounds fine," he said dispassionately.

"Fine?" I asked, squinting at him. "Just fine? You're going to spend a fortune on *fine*?"

Dick examined me like I was something distasteful he

would scrape off the bottom of his shoe. I felt hurt and embarrassed. I handled it by getting pissed.

"Lay it out," I snapped. "Show your cards now. If you're trying to set me up to fail, be man enough to tell me. If we're playing a game, it's only fair to state the rules."

"Not a game," he replied.

"Sounds like one to me."

He shrugged. For the second time during the meeting, I sat on my hands. This time I wanted to throat punch him. That seemed excessive. He was also huge and certifiable. My gut told me he wouldn't retaliate physically. According to him, he was here to *protect* me... However, even though the contract was signed, he could pull the plug if I assaulted him.

Until I met Dick, I wasn't a violent person. I mean, I had violent thoughts just like any normal person. However, Dick made me seriously want to act on them. The whack-job brought out all of my baser instincts.

"The *game* has already been revealed," he said. "You choose not to embrace the truth. Not my problem. Wait. I stand corrected." He ran his hands through his hair and made a sound of disgust. "Unfortunately, you're my problem."

I groaned. We were clearly back to the Demon thing. His crazy was showing. "So let me get this straight," I said, wondering if I went along with his fantasy if I could make my life a little easier. "You're about to spend a ton of moolah because you and I are Demons?"

"Correct."

Chill bumps popped up all over my body. The conversation was bizarre on every level. "Mmkay," I went on as Dick continued to stare at me with an expression of amused disdain. "Because we're both the same... umm... species, you want to help me?"

"Hardly," he said with a harsh laugh. "You're an assignment. Trust me, I don't want to be here."

My hands clenched into fists under my rear end. It wasn't comfortable, but I couldn't stop my visceral reaction. A bruised butt was preferable to losing the show or getting arrested for attempted murder.

What the hell was happening to me? I didn't recognize myself. The feeling was close to debilitating and left me breathless and depressed.

I sighed. My chin dropped to my chest. The overwhelming need to cry consumed me. I sucked it back. Dick would use and abuse any sign of weakness. Of that, I was sure. My mind raced with terrible and heartbreaking scenarios. The saying "beware of what you wish for" danced across my frontal lobe as I fought with myself silently. The end game was never like one imagined. I heard my heartbeat in my ears and I was glad I was seated. My legs felt like noodles.

I was done.

Mariah was going to shit a brick, but I knew deep in my soul if I got involved in Dick's game, my life would change forever… and not in a good way. Finding a job for Jenni would be a piece of cake. She was the best in the business, and Sushi most likely already had tons of offers coming in. Financially, I didn't need to work. With Man-mom's investments and Sean's ongoing successful love affair with the stock market, plus residuals from *Camp Bite*, I was set for life.

I kept working because it fed my soul and gave me purpose. It was my reason and my passion. Too bad, so sad. In the scheme of life, I had it good.

I'd just have to find a new purpose. The thought was strange. It felt like I was cutting off a body part. Dramatic? Yes. Did my melodramatic tendencies matter? Nope. My self-respect and newfound self-preservation instincts had just kicked in with a vengeance. The decision felt akin to life or death. I came close to laughing at my thoughts, but laughter wasn't the right reaction. Throwing a tantrum might help, but that wasn't my style. Never had been. Never would be.

"I'll pass," I said quietly. "Rip up the contract. I can't do this."

Dick rolled his eyes. "I figured you for a lot of things, but not a quitter."

I raised a brow and laughed. The sound was humorless and frigid. "You don't know me at all," I said coldly. "But here's what I know about you. You need help. I don't like you, but I can feel compassion for you because I'm a decent human being —*not a Demon*. You've obviously been through something traumatic. I'm truly sorry about that." I actually meant it. I wasn't a monster. And I had no intention of working with one, even though he held the key to the magic I'd long searched for.

I sighed and looked straight at him. "I won't breathe a word of your delusions to anyone, and I'll make you a list of reputable therapists and psychiatrists. Please talk to someone. I think it might help. If you want me to, I'll call and make your first appointment. It would give me peace of mind to know you won't behave this way to anyone else."

Dick's mouth dropped open. I couldn't tell if he was moved or furious. Didn't matter. I'd said my piece.

Standing up, I crossed the room and offered him my hand. He stared at it and didn't move a muscle. His eyes raised to mine. His expression was one I couldn't decipher to save my life. I kept my gaze glued to his. Honestly, I couldn't have looked away if the building had blown up. It was sexual, uncomfortable and terrifying. The unsettling sensations that ripped through my body further convinced me that I'd just made the right decision.

Abaddon/Abe/Dick was bad news.

"I don't accept," he finally said. "You signed. You're stuck. And trust me, the contract is ironclad."

It was my turn to go slack-jawed. "Are you serious?" I hissed.

"No," he shot back. "I'm not Serious. According to you, I'm Dick. However, the contract stands. Period."

"Why?" I shouted. "This is absurd. I could tank the entire project on purpose and cost you millions."

He shrugged. "Get this through your obviously thick head, Cecily. I could give a shit about the TV show. I don't even own a TV," he informed me. "I have to protect your life. Having you under my thumb is the easiest way to do it. The end."

"Oh my God," I choked out on a hysterical laugh, trying to grab the contract and tear it up.

I was fast. Dick was faster. He held it out of my reach and grinned.

"Fuck you," I snapped.

"It could be arranged," he replied suggestively.

I blew out an explosive burst of air. Going to jail didn't sound so bad anymore. Landing in the rags wouldn't affect me. I was getting out of the biz. It would be easy to convince Sean and Man-mom to move to a hidden compound in the mountains of Colorado. Pot was legal there. Sean would be all in. Man-mom could paint cockroaches anywhere. Dead Uncle Joe would love being naked in the wilderness. If I remembered correctly, his nudist colony had been in Colorado. Win-win.

There was no doubt I'd lost it. Considering my dead uncle's feelings about my new property purchase was solid proof.

Diving across the desk, I went for Dick's eyes. If I gouged him, I could get to the contract and destroy it. My thinking was muddled and screwed up, but I was working on adrenaline, a chimichanga and half a margarita. All I knew was that what I was doing felt all kinds of right even though somewhere in the back of my brain I knew it was incredibly wrong.

"There she is," Dick said with a laugh as he intercepted my attack, flipped me around and pulled me onto his lap. My arms were trapped at my sides.

"Let me go," I snarled, trying in vain to wiggle out of his embrace.

"Not a chance," he replied. "Listen to me carefully, Cecily." His breath was hot against my ear. "You're a Demon. I'm a Demon. Your mother, Lilith, is a Demon Goddess of Hell—one of two. The Underworld, aside from Satan—who's more of a concept than a person—and the Grim Reaper—who is definitely a person, is a matriarchal society. The goddesses run the show. A female offspring of a goddess is a rare and unheard of occurrence—one that would cause the power to shift. Shifting the power of beings who can destroy the Universe is a bit of an issue."

I listened. I didn't have much of a choice. It was an interesting story, but it had some major plot holes. "Okay," I ground out. "Let's pretend I buy the bullshit. It makes no sense that you would want me alive. To avoid Armageddon, it seems a whole lot easier to just off me."

I couldn't believe I was making an argument for my own demise, but I needed to point out that the tale didn't hold water. I was a stickler for stories that made sense.

"I argued that point myself," Dick admitted. "However, I'm loyal to Lilith and not the bitch who wants her dead—hence *you* dead. I'm doing the bidding of my goddess. There is *nothing* I would not do for her."

"Nothing?" I inquired sarcastically.

"Absolutely nothing," he shot right back.

My body clenched, and the most ugly and inappropriate thoughts obsessed me. Dick was in love with my mom. It icked me out majorly and infuriated me at the same time. I might need a straightjacket more than Dick. First off, I still didn't believe any of the story. So, my jealousy that Dick the Demon had a thing for my Demon goddess mom who didn't want me was beyond ridiculous.

Words escaped me. Processing the gross thoughts in my mind was all I had energy for.

"I'll release you if you promise not to attack me again," Dick said with his lips still pressed against my ear.

His voice was like foreplay. My back was against his hard chest and his arms were like a vise around me. However, the most alarming sensation was his physical attraction, which was undeniable since I was sitting on top of it. The man who said he was a Demon and all but admitted he was banging my egg donor had a whopper of an erection for the daughter of the gal he was intimate with. The most horrifying thing, though, was the fact that my girly bits were all for the disgustingly improper situation.

While I wasn't sure I could keep myself from attacking him again, I had to get off of Dick's lap. His *dick* made our physical circumstances beyond awkward.

"I won't attack," I whispered. "Just let me leave."

Slowly his grip loosened, and I dove away. I landed in a heap on the floor. If I really was a Demon, which I wasn't, this would be the point in the action where I would disappear in a hail storm of magical fire.

Instead, I was just a lump of a loser on an expensive beige rug.

And then all Hell broke loose. Literally.

CHAPTER EIGHT

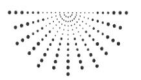

The door to Dick's office burst open with a crash that made me jump and the hair on the back of my neck stand up. The searing heat that arrived with the four intruders made me feel lightheaded and sick to my stomach. The putrid smell of sulfur hung in the air and the lighting fixtures in the office exploded. The special effects were outstanding.

Dick roared in a language I didn't understand, picked me up like I weighed nothing and put me behind him. Peeking out from behind his massive frame, I wasn't sure whether to laugh or scream. My entire body shook with fear. Part of me wanted to dive out of the floor-to-ceiling windows and run for my life, and the other part wanted to pull out my cellphone and record the performance unfolding. Jenni would crap her pants at how real it seemed.

Dick was brilliant. He'd created a scene to scare me into believing that Demons did indeed exist. If that was the case, he was crazier than I'd originally thought. The four hulking men with Goat Eyes were literally on fire—green fire with icy-blue sparks flying off their enormous bodies. I wasn't sure how the stunt was pulled off. It appeared the fire was coming from their bare skin. Pyrotechnic movie magic had greatly improved if this was the new technology.

"Out," Dick snarled. "Not your territory. Mine. You have one minute to leave or pay the consequences."

"Territories cease to exist when the one who could destroy all still breathes," the man in the front growled. "Give us the spawn. No one else will be harmed if we get what we've come for."

The man's voice sounded like he'd swallowed broken glass—rough and terrifying. I made an educated guess that I was the *spawn* who fire-guy was talking about. The script was kind of cheesy. Dick was going to be a soprano shortly for this stunt.

"She's mine," Dick ground out in a vicious tone. "You now have thirty seconds."

I shuddered. Dick was a scary MoFo. Even the actors playing Demons appeared nervous and fearful. Dick was wasting his time as an exec. He should be an action hero. He was insanely believable and handsome enough to be a movie star. I planned to tell him once the exhibition was over. Maybe pretending to be other people would help him with his delusions. It had helped me get through my feelings of abandonment about my mother.

The fire guys drew flaming swords from their hips. It was uncannily familiar to the story my dad told last night. I half expected Dick to clap his hands, conjure up his own fire sword and lop their heads off.

And then he did.

Shit had just gotten very real.

It was bloody, fierce and fast. Dick moved so quickly, he literally disappeared for a moment. I hid behind his desk and watched with my mouth hanging open. His moves were balletic, precise and deadly. There was no way this was an act, and I swallowed back my bile, watching in horror and fascination as Dick's sword connected with the flaming freaks. The sounds as the heads of the intruders hit the ground would stay with me for a while… like forever.

One by one, each of the Demons went down. The shock on their faces right before they took their last breath was almost comical… but it wasn't at all funny.

Blood and guts smoldered in piles on the floor and the smell was grotesque. Dick kicked the heads of the invaders like they were soccer balls and hissed words in the unfamiliar language he'd spoken when they arrived.

"Are you alright?" he asked with his back still turned to me.

"Umm…" I wasn't sure how to answer.

Dick glanced over and assessed me for damage. Outwardly there was none. Inwardly was another story. With a wave of his hand, the men's headless bodies turned to dust. With a few more exotic-sounding spoken words, the entire room went back to its former ornate glory before the flaming men had busted through the door.

That's when I passed out.

∼

"WHERE AM I?" I WHISPERED, RUBBING MY EYES AND GLANCING around in confusion.

I was in a bedroom—a distinctly male bedroom. The sheets were soft and a muted green in color. The thread count was seriously high. The silk duvet was navy and the bed itself was the most comfortable one I'd ever lain on. I inhaled deeply and made an attempt to calm my racing thoughts. My head hurt and my mind was jumbled. Trying to remember my dream was difficult. My God, had I tied one on and gone home with some random guy who had great taste in bedding?

I wasn't that kind of girl. I mean, I wasn't a prude by any stretch of the imagination, but all of my adult relationships had taken place with people I'd gotten to know and like first. Most of them had turned out to be jackasses, but they hadn't started out that way. Alcohol was not involved in my romantic decisions. I'd learned that lesson the hard way. My three-month marriage to Slash Gordon was proof.

"What the fu…?" I muttered, squinting at the walls in the room.

They were a dark taupe and covered with paintings… my dad's paintings. All scenes from the Underworld. Even the piece Sean had mentioned, the one I'd missed with Bozo the Clown juggling hellhounds with that skeleton dude, Charon, offering him a ferry ride into Hell.

Bizarre.

Slipping out of the bed, I looked out of the window. The sun was setting and my dream, which I was ninety-five percent sure hadn't been a dream, came roaring back. The smell of sulfur on my pretty and now very wrinkled Alice and Olivia dress was proof. I was glad I hadn't paid full price. I was going to have to trash it.

I was at Dick's house. I would bet the hidden family compound in Colorado that I planned to buy on it.

"Dick," I yelled as I slipped into my shoes. "Where are you?"

No answer.

If at first you don't succeed… "Abaddon, show your ugly ass," I shouted.

"You rang?" he asked, standing in the doorway of the room. He'd changed. Jeans and a t-shirt that hugged his stupid body had replaced the suit. He wore casual as well as he wore formal. The man was so good-looking it should be illegal.

Shoving him out of the way and marching out of the bedroom because it felt too personal, I made my way through a maze of hallways to what appeared to be the living room. It had a feel of casual elegance except for the scarily tacky life-size vase of Dolly Parton and Ron Howard playing poker with the Devil.

Well, now I knew who was buying Man-mom's art. Why, was the question.

"Have a seat, Cecily," Dick said, walking over to a fully stocked bar. "Wine or something stronger?"

"Coke. Full sugar," I snapped, refusing to sit. This wasn't a friendly visit. I wasn't even sure how I got here. Did Dick carry me out of the studio thrown over his shoulder after he'd beheaded the fire freaks? That would have raised a few eyebrows and started tongues wagging. I reminded myself that it didn't matter. I wasn't an actress anymore. What the gossips thought about me wasn't my problem.

But I was beginning to believe that I had other problems… big ones.

"That was real? In the office?" I asked, taking the Coke from his hand and sucking back a healthy chug.

"Very," he replied, seating himself comfortably on the leather couch and sipping on something amber.

"You killed four men?"

"Demons," he corrected me. "It was them or you. I chose you."

I stared at him for a long moment. "Because you had to."

He shrugged and refused to answer. Didn't matter. He'd made himself and his feelings about me abundantly clear.

"How did I get here and is this your house?"

He nodded. "It's my house. It's down the street from yours," he said. "And we got here the same way we went to Hell. We transported."

I swallowed back my sarcastic reply. I was beginning to believe him, which meant I was close to a psychotic break.

"I want to go home," I said, beginning to shake. The reality of what had almost happened was too much. Wrapping my mind around the truth that my dad and Dick had tried to impart might end me. "I want Man-mom and Sean."

"Not yet," Dick said. "We need to talk."

I nodded. I didn't have the energy to argue. My world as I'd known it was spiraling out of control. I still had a few suspicions in the back of my mind that what had happened was some kind of nefarious plan to make me think I was insane, but that reality was looking mighty slim.

"You're a real Demon?" I asked woodenly.

"I am."

"And I'm a Demon," I said flatly.

"You are," he replied.

"And everyone wants me dead?" I asked, wanting to get it all straight.

"No, there's a small faction who know of you. They want you dead. Most are not aware of your existence and we're trying to keep it that way."

Again, I nodded. I'd never been one to believe in ghosts or the supernatural even though I'd played a vampire on TV for a good portion of my childhood. I wasn't even sure what I thought about Heaven and Hell. Man-mom hadn't been into organized religion and I'd only stepped foot into a church once in my life.

I barked out a hollow laugh and wondered if I'd been in danger of combusting. Being a Demon in the House of God was probably a bad move. The simple fact that I'd just thought of myself as a Demon felt strangely and alarmingly right.

"I liked Hell," I muttered, shaking my head.

"Nothing not to like," Dick commented.

I glanced up at him. I'd forgotten he was here. "I have questions."

"Ask."

He walked over to the bar and topped off his drink. It was bourbon. He also got me another soda. Sitting back down on the couch, he crossed his jean-clad legs and waited.

"I have a million," I warned him, sitting down on the very edge of the leather chair across from him. I was not going to make myself at home. This was not my home and Dick was not my friend. "Do I have one of those fire swords?" I asked.

He laughed.

I flipped him off.

"Eventually," he replied cagily. "You have to be trained."

"So, Demons don't automatically come with the sword?"

Dick pressed the bridge of his nose and sighed dramatically. "No. No, they don't. It can take a very long time before a Demon is experienced or powerful enough to wield a fire sword."

I stared at him as a thought occurred to me. "How old are you?"

"Irrelevant," he replied.

I rolled my eyes. Dude was old. He didn't look a day over forty-five. For a hot sec I wondered if I would stop aging. Probably not. I was only half Demon. "Fine. How did the other goddess in Hell find out about me?"

"Good question, and one that I don't have the answer to," he told me. "However, that too is irrelevant since the knowledge is out there."

"What you're telling me is that I have a bounty on my head. Correct?"

"Correct."

I got up and paced the room. Fine. Information was knowledge. I'd just bought property in the Straightjacket Subdivision. I was ready to move the furniture in.

"Oh my God. You've been sent here against your will to protect me because you're banging my mother," I muttered under my breath.

Dick choked on his bourbon. "I'm sorry, what did you just say?"

"Nothing," I snapped. "And you know what? We can skip that one. It's none of my business. What I need to know is if you'll train me. I think you're an asshole, and the sooner I can learn how to protect myself from flaming giants, the sooner you can go back to Hell."

Dick was stunned to silence. I wasn't sure if it was because I'd busted on him for banging my mother or that I'd called him an asshole. Didn't matter.

"You can't take on a Demon," he finally said.

"I call bullshit. From what you explained, my mother—for lack of a better term—is a Demon Goddess. I would guess that I got her genes. Isn't that why I'm a wanted woman?"

Again, Dick wasn't sure how to respond. He put down his drink and scrubbed his hands over his face. "Didn't expect this," he muttered.

"I'm full of surprises, Dick."

His head fell back on his shoulders and he stared at the ceiling. "I thought we'd moved on from Dick to Abaddon."

"You thought wrong."

"I can see that. So be it. When you're not working on the

show, I'll train you," he conceded. "There are others in this realm as well who might be willing to help."

"I'm not doing the show."

He smiled. It was lopsided and every kind of sexy. I looked away.

"You signed a contract," he reminded me. "You'll be doing the show."

I'd about had it with being told what to do by an idiot who had a flaming sword and was probably older than dirt. Yep, I was playing with fire, but chances were good that I was going to get offed soon anyway.

"Plans have changed," I informed him. "I'm moving to the wilds of Colorado where pot is legal, no one can find me and my dead uncle can be nude all the time. You will be given the address and can train me when you're not working at the studio. You won't have to fly since you can poof around."

"Your dead uncle?" he questioned with a raised brow.

"Yes," I hissed. "You have a problem with dead nudists?"

He didn't answer me. I didn't blame him. It was a bizarre question. "It's a solid plan for me to go into hiding."

"It's a shitty plan," Dick announced, annoyed as all get out. "I just bought a fucking studio to be able to protect you while you get to do what you love."

"Wait. What?" I asked. That was a nice thing to do. Dick wasn't nice. Dick hated me.

"I retract most of what I just said," he ground out. "However, I did buy Keystone. You *are* doing the damn show."

I smiled. Dick had just played a hand that he didn't want me to see. Maybe he was nicer than he wanted to let on. Probably not, but one could pretend. I was excellent at pretending.

"You don't hate me," I said, wanting to piss him off.

"Dream on," he replied coldly.

I laughed. I'd lost my mind and was going with it.

I was a Demon.

I was a Demon with a bounty on my head through no fault of my own.

Dick was my reluctant bodyguard.

Dick was going to teach me how to defend myself.

I was ready to plant flowers in the Straightjacket Subdivision.

"You win… this one," I said. "I'll do the show. It's going to cost the studio a fortune to make it happen so fast. However, if we're going to work and train together, you have to stop being such a dick… Dick."

"Do you really have to call me Dick?" he asked with a grimace.

"Here's the deal, *Dick*," I said, extending my hand. "When you stop being a dick for at least seventy-two hours straight, I'll stop calling you Dick."

He chuckled and took my hand in his. Tingles shot up my arm at his touch. I schooled my face to show nothing. I really didn't need my mother's sex buddy to know how he affected me. I was grossed out enough that I felt anything. It was my icky secret to keep. And keep it, I would.

"Deal," he said. "You want to go home now?"

"Yes," I said, then paused. "Am I safe there?"

He nodded curtly. "You are. The entire street has been magically warded. No Demons other than you and me are permitted to enter unless I allow it."

"Who did that?" I asked.

"Your mother," he replied.

This time I nodded curtly. While the protection was appreciated since I would lose my shit if my brother or father got caught in the crossfire of the flaming jackasses out to kill me, I would not be thanking my mother anytime soon. She'd had forty years to check in and she hadn't. I would have kept her existence a secret. I would have protected the secret with my life.

Now it was looking like I was going to lose my life and I'd never even had the precious secret to protect.

Her loss. I was a great freaking person.

"Take me home." My tone was icy.

Dick observed me with interest, but didn't comment. He was a smart Demon. Fire sword or no, if he needled me about getting to know my mother or thanking her for anything, I'd buy a blowtorch and light his ass on fire.

I might not be powerful enough to clap my hands and conjure up a purple sword… yet. But I had credit cards and I knew how to use them. Maybe I'd go online and order a blowtorch tonight—possibly twelve.

I smiled.

I was nuts, but I never did anything halfway. If I was a Demon, I would be the most badass Demon in existence.

Or, I'd be six feet under with Uncle Joe next week.

It was fifty-fifty.

CHAPTER NINE

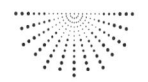

My house was empty. The peace and safety I'd once felt in my home was gone. Hell, the peace and safety I'd felt in life had evaporated for good a few hours ago. Whatever. Life goes on… at least for the moment.

It was too late in the evening to call Sean and Man-mom. It was a no-brainer that I could wake them up and they'd be right over, but I needed to process everything. After ordering a dozen blowtorches online, I took a long, scalding hot shower to wash the horrible day off of my body then put on comfy, ratty old sweatpants and a t-shirt.

Dick had walked me down the street to my house after our *chat*. Not a single word had been exchanged. The asshole lived five houses down. Same side of the street. I wanted to ask how long he'd lived there, but refrained. Knowledge wasn't always comforting. From the looks of the décor filled with my dad's artwork, my guess would be a while.

Again, whatever.

"Why don't I have a dog or a cat?" I asked my empty living room. Some unconditional love would be amazing right now.

"Don't think you're home enough for a dog," a voice said. "A cat would be a better bet. I had a cat. Named it Frank. Found out Frank had a vagina after about six years, but it was too late to change the damn name. Pretty sure that's why Frank attacked me regularly."

I screamed and grabbed a lamp as a weapon. With all the shrieking I'd done lately it was a shame I wasn't rehearsing for a horror film. Unfortunately, my real life was turning into a horror movie.

"Who's here?" I shouted, glancing around wildly.

The voice had sounded vaguely familiar, but I couldn't place it. It was definitely male. Had Jonny Benji Runky come to exact his revenge? It didn't sound like the drunken idiot, but I'd had a shitty few days and wasn't in top form.

"I'm calling the cops," I said, grabbing my cellphone. "If you're still here, I'd suggest leaving. NOW."

"Won't help," the voice assured me in a friendly tone. "They'll just throw you in the looney bin."

Where in the hell was the voice coming from? It sounded like he was near the couch, but there was no one there.

"Mmkay." I slowly squatted so I could peek under the couch. Nothing. If I didn't already know I was nuts, this would have put me over the edge.

If it was a Demon who wanted to kill me, my guess was that I'd already be dead. Plus, Dick had promised the area was warded. So, if the intruder wasn't an enemy, maybe he was some kind of magical help.

"Shit," I muttered with a bark of semi-hysterical laughter. "The looney bin might be the right place for me."

"No, no, no," the voice said. "You're as right as rain. Always have been."

"What?" I asked.

"Just letting you know, you're a sensible young gal."

"Debatable," I muttered, still scanning the room. I had no clue as to why I wasn't terrified, but I wasn't. Famous last thoughts before a grisly murder…

"How about we play the guessing game?" the voice suggested.

"Why not?" I kept my finger poised above the cellphone. The smart thing to do would be to call the cops. However, my gut told me to wait. My gut was probably going to get me killed, but it might be better to die by the hand of someone who seemed nice than one of the flaming Demons I'd witnessed earlier.

My reasoning process was warped. Go figure.

"Go ahead," the voice encouraged. "Guess who I am! It will be fun."

I shook my head and tried not to smile. I failed. Unsure if our definitions of fun matched, I played along. When the chances were good that my world might end shortly, I may as well go out playing a game. "Fine. Do I know you?"

"Oh yes!"

Again, the voice sounded familiar. It was definitely male and on the much older side. "Have we worked together?"

I'd worked with a lot of people over the years. Remembering all of them would be next to impossible, but it was a place to start.

"Nope," he replied.

Crap. Where in the heck was he hiding? Had to be behind the curtains. However, there was no bulge in the curtains. Was he a little person?

"Umm… are you tall or short?"

"Interesting question," he replied. "Used to be about five-foot-eleven. I've shrunk a bit."

Bizarre. He must be old. "Your age?"

"Oh my goodness! That's a rude question," he pointed out.

I rolled my eyes. "It's the guessing game. You broke into my house," I reminded him. "I get to ask whatever I want."

"Fair enough. Seventy-five last year," he replied.

"So, you're seventy-six now?"

"Sure," he replied noncommittedly. "One could say that."

This was utterly ridiculous. "Are you here to kill me?" I demanded, getting to the important part.

"Goodness, no! I'm a pacifist. Wouldn't harm a fly," he insisted.

Because I was clearly insane, his answer worked very well for me. I decided to believe him. If he did end up decapitating me at least we were on friendly terms. "Are we friends or acquaintances?"

"*Much more* than simply friends or acquaintances," he said with a chuckle.

I scrunched my nose. Gross. I was positive I had not banged a man in his seventies. Nor in my younger and wilder years had I banged anyone over fifty. This entire conversation was getting iffy.

"Where are you hiding?" I demanded. I was exhausted. We needed to get to the end of the game and he needed to leave. While it didn't seem like he was a Demonic assassin, I wasn't in the mood for a geriatric stalker. I'd had several—mostly those who secretly thought they were vampires and were obsessed with *Camp Bite*.

"I'm not," he said.

"Not what?" I asked, confused.

"Not hiding, Cecily," he clarified.

I was about to give up. "I'm at a disadvantage here. You

seem to know who I am—which makes sense since you broke into my house—but I have no clue who you are."

He giggled. The sound was bizarre. The invisible weirdo was as nutty as I was.

"Would you like a hint?"

I blew out a long and very audible breath. I hated not winning, but I was going to fall asleep soon and whoever he was needed to go home. "Yes," I conceded. "But not a really good one. Make it vague. Don't give it away on the first hint."

Again, he giggled. Again, it was bizarre, but it was also sweet.

"Disco!"

"Disco?" I asked, pressing the bridge of my nose. "What kind of hint is that?"

"You did ask for a vague hint," he pointed out.

"True," I agreed. "Maybe, a little less vague."

"Tango," he added.

I shook my head and sighed. It had been an endless day that was morphing into an endless night. "Another."

"Clogging!"

The man was lacking brain cells if he believed his hints were helping.

"Okay guy, I give up," I said.

"Never give up, Cecily," he shared, sounding quite serious. "I never did, and you shouldn't either. Tango your way through life. Waltz during the happy times and jazz run right out of the sad times. Tap dance your troubles away and breakdance when it's your time to go."

I gasped. If there was a mirror handy, I was pretty sure I'd paled considerably. This was impossible.

Wait.

I was a *Demon*. Why would I think anything was impossible?

"Did you draw a penis on Man-mom's cockroach?" I whispered.

"YES!" he bellowed with delight.

My head felt light. Sean was going to poop a cow when I told him. "But I thought you were dead."

"Ohhh, I am," Uncle Joe confirmed.

"But we're talking?" I asked, pinching myself to make sure I wasn't dreaming. I wasn't.

"We are! So thrilling! I tried and tried to talk to Bill and Sean, but no go. I knew they could feel me, so I left a little phallic message on the roach. But you! You're so special, Cecily! I just knew you would be able to see me."

"I can't," I told him. "I can hear you, but I don't see you." Which was kind of a relief since he was probably naked. "Where are you?"

"Sitting on your couch," Uncle Joe replied.

I winced. "Naked?"

"Definitely."

Shit. I wasn't sure if a ghost could leave skid marks, but the thought was horrifying. I loved my couch. Shaking my head, I pushed the graphic images away. I also loved my uncle. But why was he here? "Umm... so, is there no Heaven?"

Uncle Joe was quiet for a long moment. "I don't rightly know," he said. "If there is, I'm not there."

This was all kinds of off. Uncle Joe was whacky, but he was a very good and kind man. Maybe, Heaven didn't exist. That didn't stand to reason. I'd just been on a possibly drug-induced trip to Hell with Dick. If there was a Hell, there must be a Heaven.

"Okay," I said, not wanting to upset my dead uncle. "No

worries. I have plenty of room. You can have the spare bedroom and tomorrow I can interpret for you so you can talk to Man-mom and Sean."

"Wonderful!" Uncle Joe sang. "I'm doing moves from *Saturday Night Fever* right now. I so wish you could see me, Cecily."

I was seriously glad I couldn't. Naked disco wasn't my thing. "Me too, Uncle Joe," I lied. "I need to make some ground rules if we're going to be roommates."

"Absolutely!" Uncle Joe said, sounding winded. He must've been dancing up a naked storm.

"My bathroom is off limits," I told him. "No sneaking up on me, please. I'm a little on the unstable side right now."

"Would you like to talk about it?" Uncle Joe asked kindly. "I'm a very good listener."

I smiled. It was a real smile. The situation was beyond absurd, but his love for me was obvious and true. I'd take it. "Maybe tomorrow. I'm really tired."

"Then I say we hit the sack, niece of mine," Uncle Joe announced. "Tomorrow is a new day. The sun will come out tomorrow. Bet your bottom dollar!"

"Should I call you Annie?" I asked with a half-laugh/half-groan.

"Didn't know if you would get the reference," he said with a chuckle.

"Would have been hard to miss," I pointed out.

"Broadway musicals aside, my words are genuine. Every day is a new beginning. A fresh start."

I was tempted to add it was also potentially a day to get murdered by Demons, but I didn't want to jack up his happiness. "Thanks, Uncle Joe. Hope you can stay for a while."

"Me too! Now go to bed, child. I'm just going to dance a bit more and I'll soon follow."

"To the guest room," I reminded him. I loved my uncle but didn't want to share a bed with his naked self, even if he was dead and invisible. It was bad enough that his bare ghostly ass had been on my couch.

"But of course!"

I groaned as I crawled into bed. I didn't wash my face. I didn't remove my contact lens that covered my birth defect that had turned out to be way more than a strange eye. I didn't brush my teeth. I didn't care. All I wanted to do was sleep.

It was a little concerning that Uncle Joe was not in Heaven. But then again, maybe that was common. Maybe people stuck around for a while before they left this realm. Or… maybe Uncle Joe was here to stay. Things could be far worse. He was a great guy—naked or clothed.

According to Uncle Joe, every day was a new beginning. A fresh start.

That was my new motto. I was sticking to it.

CHAPTER TEN

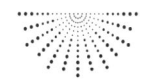

The day had dawned sunny and warm—typical California weather. My mood didn't match, but I was trying. As Uncle Joe had wisely shared last night, it was a new day—a fresh start. The past few days had been bad to put it mildly. Sending good juju out into the Universe, I prayed that today would break the shitty streak.

"One can always hope," I muttered as I focused on the work in front of me. My kitchen table was covered in documents. Important and life-changing pieces of paper.

The spread sheets that Mariah had sent over were giving me a headache. No. I stand corrected. Uncle Joe asking Alexa to play "Physical" by Olivia Newton John on repeat for the last hour was the culprit of the frontal lobe pain I was experiencing. From the sound of the huffing and puffing, he was gettin' down in a big bad way.

Thankfully, I couldn't see the show. That would have made me upchuck my hardboiled egg. I was back on the eating healthy kick. Sean was going to have to remove all the carbs from my house. I wasn't strong enough to do it without throwing a fit. If I was going to shoot a pilot in a few weeks, I needed to be in fighting form.

I'd been up since five in the morning fleshing out the concept. The stories I had from my own experiences—the good, bad and seriously ugly—were going to become comedic gold. I'd typed so much, so fast, that I was pretty sure I had most of the first season mapped out, starting with the soap opera nightmare. I needed to show it to Sean. I would kill to have my brother in the writing room, but he was more into poetry than the sitcom format. However, I had plans to pick his brilliant brain.

All the names of the innocent and guilty had been changed. I wasn't a dummy. Lawsuits were not part of the equation. When I envisioned the show in my mind, I realized I didn't want a studio audience sitcom. It would be all wrong. I loved the look of single-camera shows and I knew I wanted Bean Gomez to be the director of photography. She was brilliant, around forty-five and had an eye for comedy that was unparalleled. The DP didn't come cheap, but I didn't have budget limitations. Dick was probably going to live to regret that move. I didn't care. The chances of me staying alive for another year were looking slim. If I was going to bite it, I was going to win an Emmy first—even if it was posthumously.

"Should you call the guys?" Uncle Joe asked, huffing and puffing.

"Nope," I replied, not looking up. Granted there was nothing to actually see, but I was trying to decipher the finances Mariah had sent. Shockingly, the fact that I was talking to my deceased uncle didn't faze me. There were plenty of reality shows about the paranormal—not that I watched any, but if they were that popular there had to be something to them. Speaking of, I'd seen Dick decapitate guys spitting fire from their skin. A sweet dead relative was a vast improvement over that shitshow. "It's seven in the morning, Uncle Joe. Man-mom gets up at eight and Sean's been known to sleep until noon. I'll call at nine."

"Works for me," he said. "I feel the need to commune with nature. Yoga in the backyard under the lemon tree is the answer! Would you like to join me, Cecily?"

I smiled in the direction of the invisible dead man. "Nope. I have to work. Maybe another time."

"Namaste," he called out as he did whatever ghosts do to leave a house.

I paused and took a sip of my coffee. In a matter of two days, I'd been humiliatingly fired, gone to Hell, given the chance of a lifetime with the new show, was almost killed by Demons, made a semi-truce with the hot Demon who was banging my absentee mom and had gained a dead roommate. Oh, and I was a denizen of the Underworld apparently.

Good times.

"I probably should have gotten high and gone to the airport with Sean to watch the underside of planes," I muttered, going over the list of writers Mariah had submitted.

They were the best of the best. It made me tingly. The magic was back. My agent had made notes that everyone in Hollywood was interested and chomping at the bit to snag a position. It was unreal. Going from the lowest of lows, and showing my *not* bootylicious butt to the network suits, to the top of the food chain was staggering.

There was part of me that felt like a fraud. I didn't land the deal because Keystone believed in my talent and thought I could carry a show. I'd gotten the sweetest deal known to man because Dick was tasked with keeping me alive.

Thankfully, no one but Dick and me knew that unsavory bit of information.

Did it matter? Jonny Benji Runky sucked and had a show. I didn't suck, and I'd make damn sure the cast, crew and writing staff were killer. I wasn't an egotistical asshole. I was a hardworking actress who wanted to live the magic and tell stories. So, no. It didn't matter how the opportunity came about. What mattered was what I did with it.

Quickly dialing Mariah, I put her on speakerphone. I valued and needed my hearing skills.

"Baby," Mariah shouted. "I LOVE YOU! Did you get the paperwork I had messengered over?"

"I did," I said, feeling truly excited. "I want Bean Gomez as DP. Jenni Gallagher as head of hair and makeup, and Sushi as costume designer. Pay them their quote and offer a large bonus to sweeten the deal since we're all about to give up our lives."

"Done," Mariah said. "Might have to give Bean Gomez a percentage of the show to bag her."

"Do it," I said. "I'll start out in the writer's room and then hand it off when we're on the same page. I want offers to go out to Rick Gee, Jameson Kall, Georgia Nagel and Kristen Calvert."

"Pretty sure my grundies are soaked," Mariah yelled gleefully.

I winced and gagged a little. "TMI."

"The truth is messy," she shot back with a cackle. "It's gonna cost us to get that group of veterans."

"No," I contradicted her. "It's going to cost Keystone."

"Orgasm. I just had a damn orgasm," Mariah wheezed out.

"Rein it in," I told her with an eye roll. "Or at the very least, keep that shit to yourself."

"Roger that," she replied.

I could literally hear her grinning.

"Do we have office space yet?" I asked, skimming the other bullet points.

"Whole floor of Building C," Mariah confirmed. "Offices are up and running now. We just need to fill them."

"Holy crap," I said as my stomach cramped. "This is really happening."

"Damn straight," she replied. "Don't think about it too deep. I learned that little gem the hard way. Had to change my underpants six times already this morning."

I actually jotted down what the insane woman had just said. It was gross, but I might be able to use it in the show. "Cast?" I asked.

"I got the list you texted. Offers are out. Aubrey Zawn's people countered."

"Pay her," I said automatically. "Question. Are we getting any pushback from the studio that the entire cast is over forty and mostly female?"

"Hell to the no," Mariah informed me at the top of her lungs. "Rumor has it all the studios are now trying to drum up a midlife miracle series. However, we're gonna beat their asses and win!"

"From your mouth…" I wondered for a hot sec if I was even allowed to reference God now that I knew I was a freaking Demon. Was I going to get electrocuted by a bolt of holy lightning? Warily glancing up at the ceiling, I sent a silent apology to the dude upstairs. I wasn't sure if I believed in God, but I wasn't taking any chances. I had too much going on right now to have both Heaven and Hell gunning for me.

Mariah was still yacking away. "Janie Stone looks like a yes, but has a conflict for the first six days."

"We can work around it," I told her. Janie Stone was a

dream. She was pushing fifty and could make an audience lose their minds with laughter with a simple quirk of her lip. Plus, we'd be buried in the writing cave for the first week. Wouldn't even need the actors until week two.

"Agree," she replied. "Sammy Sam Samuelson is a yes and Wanda Adams is a yes. You sure you want Wanda Adams? She's a fucking ball-buster."

I laughed. "She's playing a version of you."

Mariah was quiet for a long moment then screamed so loudly I was sure she woke up my entire neighborhood. "I know you don't wanna hear it, but I just had multiple Big O's."

"You're correct," I said, shaking my head. "As soon as the pilot and first episode are written, we can hold auditions for guest spots or just make offers."

"Beautiful," Mariah said. "PS, I'm having vaginal aftershocks right now."

"And on that note, I'm hanging up," I said with a groan.

"Seriously," Mariah said. "At sixty-five it's a miracle."

"Awesome. Keep on keeping on. Love you."

"Love you more!" she shouted before she hung up.

It was a new day.

It was a fresh start.

So far, so good.

∼

IT WAS NOON. MY LIVING ROOM WAS FILLED WITH THE MEN in my life. Two visible and breathing, one dead and most likely dancing. As strange and unbelievable as it was, it couldn't have been more perfect. My entire existence had become unimaginable. It was either go with it or crawl into a hole with a year's supply of donuts and hide.

I was going with it.

Maybe I'd come to realize all of us had lost our marbles. Or more possibly, I'd make peace that the impossible was indeed possible.

"I feel an epic poem coming on," Sean said with an astonished grin, throwing his arms wide. "Do you mind if I remove my clothes? I think I'll be able to get into the Uncle Joe mindset better."

"Yes, I mind," I told my brother. "Seeing your junk isn't on the agenda for today—or ever."

Sean laughed. "It's very nice junk I've been told."

"Ignoring you," I shot back, debating if I wanted a full sugared soda or water. Who was I kidding? Grabbing a Coke, I chugged it then sat down on the armchair and grinned at my dad and my brother. "Crazy, right?"

A smile lit my dad's face as he glanced around the room. "Where is he? Is he with us now?"

"I can't actually see him," I explained. "But I can hear him. Uncle Joe? You around?"

"But of course! So wonderful to see my handsome brother and nephew. Tell them that the milk and eggs in their refrigerator are past expiration date," he announced. "Also, Sean should check his Tinder app. Many ladies have swiped right."

I squinted at my brother.

"What?" he asked, alarmed.

"You're on Tinder?"

Sean's eyes grew huge, then he began to laugh. "An experiment for a poem," he assured me. "Although, I thought it was a secret one."

"Not anymore," I said with a raised brow. "And you guys need to throw out your milk and eggs. Uncle Joe said they've expired."

"By three months," Uncle Joe added. "Tell the boys they should go vegan. I'm one hundred percent vegan."

"Oh crap," I muttered, feeling terrible. "Are you still?"

"Still what, dear?" Uncle Joe inquired.

"Vegan. I mean, do dead people eat?" I asked. I had a ton of veggies in the fridge and fruit on the counter. The man must be starving and I hadn't offered him a thing. I'd even eaten my breakfast in front of him. That was an asshole move. Where in the heck did I leave my manners?

"Ohhh, no, no, no," Uncle Joe said with a chuckle. "The dead don't eat. Actually, I don't have any bodily functions anymore. Used to enjoy a good healthy BM every morning. Now? Nothing."

I breathed a small sigh of relief and decided not to pursue the BM conversation. I loved my uncle, but his bathroom habits were best left a mystery. No bodily functions meant that there were probably not any ghostly skid marks on my couch. Small wins would be taken gladly.

"I have gummies if Uncle Joe would like to imbibe," Sean offered, laying a baggie of colorful hallucinogenics on the coffee table.

"He doesn't eat anymore," I told my brother.

Sean popped a gummy into his mouth. "Bummer."

"Joe?" my dad said, looking around the room.

"I'm over here, Bill," Uncle Joe answered.

"He's next to me, Man-mom. On my right."

My dad waved enthusiastically at his dead brother. My guess would be that my deceased uncle waved back.

"So, Joe," my dad said with a smile he couldn't wipe off if he tried. "Are you here for a while or just passing through?"

"Not a clue!" Uncle Joe answered. "But if this is my final resting place, I'm quite pleased."

I laughed. "He doesn't know, but he's delighted to be with us."

Sean observed me in silence for a long moment. "Do you think you can see him because you *may*… or *may not* be a Demon?"

The thought had occurred to me. "I can't see him," I reminded my brother. "I can only hear him. And I have no clue if my newly discovered Demonic heritage is why I can communicate with Uncle Joe."

"Demon you say?" Uncle Joe asked, excited. "How delightful!"

"Umm… okay," I said, thinking that Uncle Joe might have carried a little dementia with him into the afterlife. Or he just had a fantastic attitude about everything. Maybe there was some kind of benefit to being naked for a few decades of one's life.

Not that I was going to experiment with the lifestyle. If I did it, then Sean would do it. If both of us became clothing impaired, then Man-mom would most likely give it a go. I'd have to cover all of my furniture in plastic and keep squirt bottles of disinfectant all over the place. I would think my fear of skid marks would outweigh any benefit of living twenty-four-seven in my birthday suit.

"Cecily," Man-mom asked carefully. "You believe… that you're a Demon?"

I nodded slowly. "I do." My knees got weak and I collapsed onto the armchair. Thankfully, I was positioned in a good spot. It would have sucked to drop to the floor like a sack of potatoes. Knowing in my head and admitting it out loud were entirely different. Part of me wanted to laugh and the other wanted to cry. Screaming seemed like a good middle of the road option, but I'd done a lot of that over the past couple of days. It was getting boring.

Dad hopped to his feet, wrapped his arms around me and hugged me close. "Something happened," he whispered. "Tell me, please. We're a team. You're not alone. It's not the end of the world."

"Debatable," I muttered, thinking about the smackdown in Dick's office.

"Talk to me," Man-mom insisted. "Please."

"Well," I said, gently extricating myself from my dad's embrace. I ran my hands through my hair, stood up and began to pace. "I saw the purple fire sword in action."

"Rad," Sean said, impressed.

Man-mom scrubbed his hands over his face and paled.

"Not rad," I corrected my brother. "There's a bounty on my head because of who gave birth to me. Dick was sent to protect me. I watched him kill four flaming assholes who wanted me dead."

"That statement was not politically correct," Sean said with a wince.

Man-mom slapped the back of Sean's head. I wanted to rack my idiot brother.

Instead, I rolled my eyes. "Oh my God. They were not gay—or I have no clue if they were gay. They were literally on fire and they were assholes… and now they're headless dead assholes."

Sean nodded. "My bad."

"I would say so, dumbass. I'm not homophobic," I snapped.

"It's a good thing you're not homophobic!" Uncle Joe announced. "Since I'm gay."

"Yes, you are," I said with a thumbs up.

Uncle Joe had never married, but I never recalled him

having a partner either. Which is why I rarely thought about his sexuality. He stood out in my memories as sweet naked Uncle Joe who danced.

"I'm what?" Sean asked, confused.

"You're an idiot. But I wasn't talking to you. I was talking to Uncle Joe. I'd forgotten he was gay."

"Of course, he's gay," Man-mom said with a nod and a warm smile in the direction of his brother. "He came out back in the sixties. Caused quite the stir."

"Oh yes. And true to form, my hero Bill is understating the event," Uncle Joe said quietly.

The mood in the room took a nosedive—not that it was great after I'd explained my near miss with death. I'd never heard the story of Uncle Joe's coming out before, but I could hear the pain in his voice. Now, I wanted to know, but only if he and Man-mom wanted to tell it. I glanced over at my dad, who was staring at the floor. Sean and I exchanged a look and my brother moved to sit next to my dad.

I looked at Man-mom and relayed his brother's message. "Uncle Joe says you were his hero, and that you're understating what happened when he came out."

"You want to talk about it?" Sean asked, putting his arm around Man-mom's shoulders.

Dad shook his head. "Not my story to tell. But I will say, I love my brother and have been proud of him my entire life."

"Uncle Joe?" I asked, looking toward the spot his voice had come from. "We're really good listeners…if you want to talk."

"Such a beautiful family I have," Uncle Joe mused. The smile in his voice was clear, as was the sadness.

I smiled back and waited. If he wanted to share, I would listen. If he didn't, I was still here. Always. All three of us were here for him, even if my brother and dad couldn't hear him.

Uncle Joe sighed, then spoke. "When I told our parents I was gay, I got kicked right out of the house with only the clothes on my back after our father tried his best to kill me. Our mother shouted scripture to rectify my disgusting and damned life—her words, not mine. She even called the church to see if they could perform an exorcism. Needless to say, it was not the reaction I'd hoped for." Uncle Joe stopped speaking for a moment. His breathing hitched and my stomach hurt. "Although, I shouldn't have been shocked. We didn't grow up in a loving home."

"What happened next?" I asked, wishing like heck that I could see him and give him a hug. I didn't even care that he was naked.

Uncle Joe continued. "I was sitting in the front yard, crying my eyes out, and what to my wondering eyes should appear? My brother Bill! He came flying out of the house with two black eyes, a split lip and a broken jaw. While I'd escaped with only a broken arm and a few bruises, Bill had taken the brunt of our father's rage for sticking up for me. My beautiful brother helped me up, led me to our father's car and we took off, never to lay eyes on our parents again."

I was stunned. It made sense now why my dad was not a religious person. My father was the best man I knew. My eyes filled with tears as I stared at Man-mom.

"Uncle Joe just told me the whole thing. I'm so sorry," I whispered.

Man-mom's sigh was pained.

I gave him a quick hug. "Dad, you're my hero."

"Mine too!" Uncle Joe added. "We drove from Ohio to California and never looked back. Ditched the car in Vegas, got our medical needs taken care of at a shelter, then hitchhiked the rest of the way to California after we'd healed up."

"Holy shit. Ohio to California," I muttered, trying to figure out how old my dad would have been. "You had to have been—"

"Sixteen," Man-mom said. "I was sixteen."

"So confused," Sean mumbled. "Someone needs to enlighten me before the high kicks in."

"May I?" I asked both Man-mom and Uncle Joe.

"Of course," Uncle Joe said as my dad nodded sadly. "It's water under the bridge now, but it's our history, and both you and Sean have the right to know."

I retold the story as best I could, including the part about when they moved to California together. Sean was silent. My brother closed his eyes and shook his head. "What is wrong with people?" he asked. "Hatred is taught, it's not innate."

"Fear," Man-mom stated. "Fear and lack of empathy do terrible things to even good people. They raised us the same way their parents raised them. I vowed never to repeat what they'd done."

"And you didn't," I said, still absorbing what my dad and his brother had experienced. "But I'd have to argue the *good people* part."

"Sometimes understanding what's foreign is difficult—impossible for some," Uncle Joe said. "Considering the time and the circumstances, they did the best they were capable of."

"Lacking," I commented. Uncle Joe might have forgiven them, but that didn't mean I had to. I'd never met them and now I knew why.

"May I suggest a game?" Uncle Joe inquired.

"A game?" I asked, confused. Games were fun. The conversation had not been fun.

"Yes," he replied. "Let's turn our frowns upside down! Your dad and I came up with the Quote Game on our cross-country drive to freedom and a new life. Helped set the path for our future."

I laughed. Man-mom had played the same game with us our entire lives. For years, I'd looked up quotes before we would play so I'd sound really smart. We'd also played the State Game and the Country Game. Sean and I had put our globe and encyclopedias to very good use. Encyclopedias were obsolete now with the internet, but we still kept the huge set out of fond memories. The books had a place of honor on Sean and Man-mom's living room bookshelf. It wasn't until we'd gotten a little older and savvier that we'd realized the games were *educational*. I'd racked up quite a few wins with the countries Nauru and Kiribati. Used to drive Sean nuts.

"Nobody actually wins the Quote Game," I said.

"Isn't that the point?" Man-mom asked, perking up at the mention of the activity. "If no one wins, then no one loses. Which means everyone wins."

I grinned at his skewed logic and shrugged. I wasn't going to argue. We could all use a win.

"Category?" Sean asked, rubbing his hands together with glee.

"Best of," Man-mom and Uncle Joe said at the same time.

Only Uncle Joe and I could hear the unison shout, but I could tell my dad felt it by his delighted chuckle.

"And the category is the best of the best quotes," I announced. "On your marks. Get set. Go!"

"Be yourself," Sean quoted. "Everyone else is taken. Oscar Wilde."

"Nice," I said. "How about a little Mae West? You only live once, but if you do it right, once is enough."

"I'll agree with that," Uncle Joe said. "For every minute you are angry you lose sixty seconds of happiness. Ralph Waldo Emerson."

I repeated Uncle Joe's contribution. Everyone loved it.

"He who angers you conquers you. Elizabeth Kenny," Man-mom added.

That one hit me in the gut, but I kept a pleasant expression on my face. Dick angered the crap out of me. He also scared the hell out of me. I needed to work that out. I had zero plans for him to conquer me. All I needed was for the Demon to teach me how to protect myself.

My brow wrinkled in thought. A horrible scenario occurred to me… would I be fighting off Demons for the rest of my life?

Stop thinking. One catastrophe at a time. I made a mental note to check with Dick on that one. Until then, it was pushed to the back of my mind.

The quotes came flying fast and furious. The game made me forget all my troubles for a good hour. Sean ordered pizza and Uncle Joe delighted in watching us eat lunch. I still felt a little guilty about that, but he assured me repeatedly that the dead don't eat.

"Last one," Sean announced, swallowing an enormous bite of pepperoni with extra cheese. "The only true wisdom is knowing that you know nothing."

"Socrates," Man-mom said.

"Correct," Sean replied.

"Very apt," Uncle Joe commented.

I agreed. My eye began to feel itchy and dry. I realized that I hadn't removed my contact lens in over twenty-four hours. Using a wet wipe to make sure there was no pizza sauce or grease on my fingers, I dug into my eye to take my disguise off.

Sean and Man-mom loved my weird eye. I figured Uncle Joe wouldn't mind. He was a great sport about everything.

"Holy shit!" I yelled.

"What?" Sean shouted, quickly shoving his bag of weed gummies down his pants. "Coppers?"

"You did not just say *coppers*," I said, not looking at him. I was still eyeing the shocking new discovery.

"My bad," he replied. "Been watching a bunch of gangster films from the thirties."

I nodded, and waved tentatively at Uncle Joe. He waved back. The man was definitely naked. He looked the same as I remembered, but parts of him were see-through and his wrinkled body was gray all over. His lifeless skin appeared papery, but it was intact. I would have thought he'd look like a decaying cadaver since he'd been dead for a year, but nope. He was just a bit transparent.

Uncle Joe's eyes grew huge. "My goodness, Cecily! Can you see me?"

I tamped back the need to toss a blanket over his bits. That would be embarrassing for him. I reminded myself that the human body was a beautiful thing—even dead, gray and somewhat see- through.

"I can see you," I said with a semi-hysterical laugh.

"Amazing!" Sean hopped to his feet and stood next to me. "Experiment."

"What?" I asked.

"Go with it," he replied, covering my Goat Eye. "Can you still see Uncle Joe?"

I couldn't. "No."

Sean then covered my good eye—or rather, the non-Goat Eye. "Now?"

"Yep," I replied, wincing a bit as Uncle Joe scratched his ghostly nuts.

"There you have it," Sean announced triumphantly. He patted me on the back. "Demons can see the dead. Congrats."

"Umm… thanks," I muttered, wondering what other bizarre things I was going to discover about myself. Hopefully, one of them would be that I did have a freaking purple fire sword. I wanted Dick out of my life as soon as possible. It was evident that the asshole felt the same.

"This is wonderful!" Uncle Joe said. "We can dance together, Cecily!"

"I don't know if dancing is a great idea. Not really much of a dancer," I told Uncle Joe.

Man-mom laughed. Sean laughed harder. I groaned just a little bit.

"Not to worry," he said. "I'm a wonderful teacher!"

"Looking forward to it," I lied.

Dancing with my dead naked uncle hadn't been in the script, but neither had learning that I was a Demon, or going to Hell and almost dying. An Oscar Wilde quote came to mind —To live is the rarest thing in the world. Most people just exist, that is all.

I had a choice. I was going to live—well, at least until an Underworld creature offed me. It occurred to me to inquire how much money a Demon would get for ending me. If it was a shit ton and my days were truly numbered, I'd think about asking Sean and Man-mom to do the honors. I'd prefer if there was some kind of benefit that it go to my family. With my dad and brother offing me, I knew it would be quick and painless. Convincing them to do it would be next to impossible, but I'd keep the plan tucked in the back of my mind.

"Shall we go outside and dance in the afternoon sun?" Uncle Joe suggested.

I grinned and grabbed my brother's and dad's hands. If I was going to dance, they were going to dance too. "Yes! I think that's a terrific idea. One hour of dancing and then I have to get back to work. Deal?"

"Deal!" Uncle Joe sang as he passed right through a solid wall and into the backyard.

I had landed in Crazytown. I was going to enjoy my stay.

CHAPTER ELEVEN

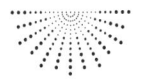

THE DANCING WAS EPIC. UNCLE JOE WAS FEELING IT. AS LONG AS I kept my eyes on his face, I could deal. Man-mom and Sean enjoyed themselves as well. Dad juggled lemons from my favorite tree and Sean demonstrated his round-off back-handspring. It was terrifying, since my brother was in his late thirties and hadn't tumbled in a decade, but he completed the trick and we didn't have to call an ambulance.

While Los Angeles wasn't what I would call a beautiful city, there were pockets of beauty everywhere. My backyard was one of those pockets. We danced to *Donna Summer's Greatest Hits* and wore ourselves out.

I was living, not existing. But now it was time to get back to work.

My living room was awash with creativity. It felt invigorating.

Sean looked over the outlines for *Ass The World Turns* that I'd written while I continued to write and send texts to Mariah. He made notes in the margins and had a few genius suggestions. Man-mom brought over an easel and canvas from next door and was busy painting a portrait of Uncle Joe. Uncle Joe sat and posed. I didn't have the heart to remind the silly old man that Man-mom couldn't see him. I explained the pose to my dad and he went to work.

"This is really damned good," Sean said, paging through my notes on the pilot. "Hilarious yet moving and timely."

"You think?" I asked as tingles tickled my stomach.

"I do," Sean replied, then focused on me. "I had no clue you could write like this, Cecily. The dialogue and timing are flat-out pro."

I grinned. "Thank you."

"Welcome, big sis," he said. "And now I'm going to say something you don't want to hear."

The tingles turned to cramps. "Speak."

"From what you explained to us, Abe is here to protect you from flaming assholes who want you dead. Correct?"

I nodded. I had no clue where he was going. With Sean it could be anywhere. It usually depended on how much jazz cabbage he had in his system.

"How many flaming assholes are after you?"

It was a good question. "Don't know," I admitted. "Dick said some knew about me and they were trying to keep others from finding out."

"Interesting," Sean said, sitting down on the floor and assuming a yoga pose.

"Interesting isn't the right word," I said flatly. "Horrifying works better."

Sean put a leg over his head. Uncle Joe joined him. I kept my eyes on my brother. Watching Uncle Joe tie himself into a knot with his wrinkled junk swaying in the breeze was simply too much to handle.

"Follow my train of thought," Sean said. "Wouldn't starring

in a TV show that's sure to be a monster hit make you more of a sitting duck for the Demons who want you dead?"

Man-mom stopped painting. Uncle Joe un-pretzeled himself and began to cha-cha nervously.

Thoughts swirled in my head. None of them good. The Demons who were aware I existed obviously knew where to find me. The street we lived on was magically warded so none of them could show up at my house. Could Dick ward the entire studio? From the shitshow I'd seen yesterday in his office, my guess was no.

"Are Dick and Abe to be trusted?" Uncle Joe asked. He'd gone from the cha-cha to the tango. It was disturbing.

"They're the same person," I told him.

"I see," he replied, confused. "But the question stands. Can he be trusted?"

"What did Joe ask?" Man-mom inquired.

"He wants to know if Dick can be trusted," I told him.

No one said a word. That didn't bode well.

"Man-mom, how long have you known Dick?" I asked.

"Since I met your mom—forty-one years ago," he replied.

"So, he was a child?" Sean asked.

"Oh no," Man-mom said with a bemused chuckle. "Abe, or Dick as Cecily prefers, is thousands of years old—possibly millions."

"Rad," Sean said.

Wrapping my head around Dick's age was going to make me tired. I didn't have time to turn something senseless into sense. "Who was he to my mother?" I asked, not really wanting to clue my dad in that Dick was banging Lilith.

Dad walked back to his easel. "Initially, I believed him to be her brother. He's not. Lilith's brother is a powerful Demon called Gideon. Quite an impressive man from the stories she told. As time went on, I learned that Abaddon was your mother's bodyguard, so to speak." His voice sounded wistful as he spoke of the happy memories of the woman he loved and clearly still did.

So to speak left so many icky options open. Lilith was dead —metaphorically speaking—to all of us. Tarnishing what she and Man-mom had would be mean. I wasn't mean. I cared nothing for Lilith, but my dad was my world.

"He lied?" I asked, beginning to wonder why I'd bought Dick's story hook, line and sinker.

"No," Man-mom said. "I made an incorrect assumption."

That was debatable. Lies by omission were still lies. Of course, the Demon part was true. No denying it. However, there was no proof that he still worked for my mother—for lack of a better word. There was no proof that he wasn't going to kill me. Maybe being on a TV show was his ploy to leave me wide open to get decapitated by a flaming asshole. Although, he had saved me from the flaming assholes in his office yesterday. Why would he do that if he wasn't trying to protect me?

Maybe it was a game for him? A *how badly can I screw with Cecily* game. One minute he's defending me, the next he's letting them cut off my head. It would make him seem innocent, as if he really had tried to protect me and failed. If he was a double agent, working for my mother *and* the other Demon who wanted me dead, then this way of taking me out would keep his hands clean.

Shit. Shit. Shit.

Just when I had a shot to make my acting dreams come true, there was a problem—a huge one. Still, running away and hiding before achieving my dreams wasn't an option I wanted to take.

"I don't want to just exist," I said. "I want to live."

"Bastardization of the Oscar Wilde quote," Sean said, impressed.

"Bingo. Look, if my days are numbered, they're numbered. If I'm going over to Uncle Joe's side then I want to go out with a bang. I want to do the show. It's every dream I've had and then some. For whatever reason—and most likely a nefarious one—Dick's given me a budget with no limitations. He bought Keystone Studios, for the love of everything absurd. He okayed the show. He says it's to protect me."

"I don't feel good about any of this," Man-mom said. "Sean made an outstanding point."

"What are the options?" I demanded. "Running away to a compound in the wilds of Colorado?"

"Easy access to pot," Sean pointed out.

"I can paint anywhere," Man-mom chimed in.

"I'd love to run naked in the woods," Uncle Joe added.

I laughed. I'd had the exact same thoughts earlier. "Nope. I'm not going to run. Dickie boy said he was going to train me."

"Again," Uncle Joe pressed. "Do we trust him?"

"Hell to the no," I said. To be honest, part of me did trust the Demon, but most of me did not. "Here's the plan. I get trained to use a purple fire sword to kill the flaming assholes who want me dead. I do the show while I learn to defend myself. Then once I can protect all of us, we take off into the wilds of Colorado. I can have my TV character killed off and the show can go on. We'll let the world think I died for real. That might throw the Demons off and we can live happily ever after. Win-win."

Sean scrunched his nose. "If Abe… I mean, Dick is a bad Demon, your butt is toast."

"Are there any good Demons?" I countered with a brow raised high.

"You're a good Demon," Sean said with a smile.

I shrugged and closed my eyes. "Not sure what else to do. If we take off now, I have no way to protect myself or you. Putting any of you in danger is not okay. Don't see that leaving immediately is a smart course of action."

Man-mom painted like his life depended on it. He created questionable works of art when he was stressed. It was what he did when he needed to think clearly. I paced. Sean did yoga. We all had our quirks.

"I'll talk to Abe," Dad finally said. "Man to man."

I didn't see that helping much, but kept my lip zipped.

"And I'll spy on him!" Uncle Joe shouted. "It's perfect. He can't see me. I can get the skinny on if he means you harm, Cecily."

I shook my head. "Dick's a Demon. He can see you. You can't spy on him. Too dangerous."

Uncle Joe looked crushed.

"Wait," Sean said, pausing his sun salutation. "Abe wears contacts like you do, right? To cover his eye?"

"Eyes," I corrected my brother. "He has two Goat Eyes. And yes, he wears contacts."

"Perfect," Uncle Joe announced in his outdoor voice. "If he's wearing the contacts, I shall spy in the open. If he's not, I will hide and spy. What's the worst that can happen if Dick catches me? I'm already dead."

Uncle Joe had a point, but it still seemed risky. "Your thinking is fairly sound. But it's a bad plan. It makes my stomach wonky."

I repeated the plan to Sean and my dad. We all thought it was a bad idea, but we all decided it was worth a shot. Uncle Joe had spent a few years in the CIA as an international spy—yet another shocking surprise about the man. However, we were going to do a test first. Having no clue if a Demon could hurt the dead didn't sit well. None of us knew how long Uncle Joe would be with us, but personally I wanted him to stay. The thought of my sweet naked uncle being harmed was unacceptable.

"I'm going to pay Dick a visit," I announced. "The dick lives down the street."

"Now?" Sean asked.

"Now," I confirmed.

"Not alone," Man-mom said, putting his paints and brushes back into his large canvas tote. "I'm coming with you."

"So am I," Sean added.

I shook my head. "Nope. Just me and Uncle Joe. I'll be able to tell if Dick can see him."

"What if he's not wearing his contacts?" Sean asked.

"Then Uncle Joe disappears. I'll just talk shop with the Demon."

My dad didn't look happy. There wasn't a whole lot to be joyous about at the moment, but standing still wasn't smart. I had no plans to let others control my destiny. I was in charge of that. If I was going to land six feet under soon, it would be on my terms.

"Can Uncle Joe disappear?" Sean inquired.

I glanced over at my dead naked relative. "That's a good question. Can you?"

"Most of the time," he replied with a laugh. "Wear a long coat. I shall hide underneath it. If Dick the dick has his contacts in, I'll slip out from under the coat and we can test the theory. We shall have a code word that the coast is clear. Disco would be good."

I repeated Uncle Joe's plan.

"Jesus," Sean said with a laugh. "It sounds like a plot from *Camp Bite*."

I didn't disagree. "Umm... how about a code word easier to work into a conversation?" I suggested.

Uncle Joe nodded. "Yes, good point. How about shimmy?"

My uncle was not good with code words.

Sean couldn't help himself. "Maybe you should gnash your fangs and Hula-Hoop."

I groaned, but smiled. "Maybe you should shut your cakehole."

"Roger that," Sean said.

I got back to the matter at hand. "How about the code word is the title of the show, *Ass The World Turns*?" I asked my uncle.

"Yes! Wonderful. Very easy to remember and rolls off the tongue beautifully."

It was hot outside. I would look like a dummy in a long coat, but I was going with it. I'd simply think of it as a costume. The thought of my bare-assed uncle smashed up against me was absurd. Whatever. My life was on the freaking line. Unsavory and bizarre measures had to be taken.

"Experiment," I said, approaching my uncle. Reaching out, I tried to take his hand. My hand went right through his. Physical touch was impossible. A part of me was sad. Hugging was out. I could have used an Uncle Joe hug—even a naked one.

"Bummer," Uncle Joe said.

I agreed. "Is what it is," I told him. "We're still together even if I can't hug you. That's what matters."

He perked right up. "Correct, my dear Cecily! And I shall be the one to save you like Bill saved me. I want to be a hero."

Smiling at the lovely old man, I gave him a thumbs up. "You're already a hero, Uncle Joe."

He chuckled. "Then I want to be a superhero. Your superhero."

"Should we pick a superhero name for you?" I asked.

Sean clapped his hands and cleared his throat. "New game! Pick a hero name for Uncle Joe. I'll start. Captain Nude-man."

Uncle Joe slapped his thigh and cackled. "Love it!"

"Agent Bare Ass or Undercover Shadow," Man-mom chimed in.

Again, Uncle Joe bellowed with laughter.

"He's loving them," I said with a giggle. "How about The Streaker Spirit?"

"Doctor Buck-Ass Naked?" Sean suggested.

Uncle Joe was laughing so hard I thought he might choke. It was a good thing he was already dead. I didn't know the Heimlich Maneuver. Not that it would work. My hands went right through my uncle.

"The Naked Phantom," Sean said. "Or Snooper Spector."

"So many wonderful titles to choose from," Uncle Joe wheezed out, still laughing. "I just don't know what to pick."

Uncle Joe's laugh was hilarious. It made me grin from ear to ear. "He's having a difficult time choosing. Loves them all."

Man-mom looked years younger than he'd been looking lately. Laughter was very good for the soul.

"I'm somewhat partial to Captain Nude-man," my dad said.

"Definitely has an excellent ring to it," Sean agreed, popping a lime-green gummy into his mouth with a grin.

"What do you think, Uncle Joe?" I asked. "You want to go with Captain Nude-man?"

"Absolutely!" he said. "However, I'd like to put a hold on Doctor Buck-Ass Naked as well. I shall happily try both of them out."

While my world might be caving in around me, my home was a happy place full of love and silliness.

"Uncle Joe is good to go with Captain Nude-man, but keeping the option of Doctor Buck-Ass Naked open."

Sean threw his head back and laughed. I realized my brother's personality was a lot like Uncle Joe's. He had a joy for life that was enviable.

"You ready to rumble, Captain Nude-man?" I asked, grabbing a long, lightweight coat out of the foyer closet.

"I am ready to rumble and rumba!"

"Let's just rumble," I told him. "Save the rumba for later."

"Roger that," Uncle Joe said.

What we were about to do was nuts. I just hoped it didn't blow up in our faces.

CHAPTER TWELVE

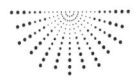

The walk to Dick's house had been too quick. I didn't feel remotely prepared. Kind of like the actor's nightmare where you find out you have to go onstage on opening night with a full audience in attendance, but realize you haven't gone to one single rehearsal. Or even worse, the nightmare where you're onstage only to glance down and discover you're naked. Uncle Joe would be fine with that one. I would not.

As stressed out as I was, I really didn't want to die. Finding out if Dick was trustworthy—as far as Demons went—was necessary. Taking him at his word was unwise. Having Uncle Joe spy didn't seem like the best way to go about it, but the choices were not many. Improv was the name of the game. I preferred a nice long rehearsal period instead of pulling it out of my ass, but my preference was irrelevant right now.

"I'm going to knock," I whispered, gathering my courage.

"Good plan," Uncle Joe whispered back. "Knock hard with authority. Be decisive. No wimpy knocks. Let Dick know you mean business."

"Okay," I said, frozen in my spot. I didn't have any idea

what I was going to talk to Dick about. I didn't want to talk to him at all. Avoiding him was better for my sanity. However, we'd concocted a plan. It was kind of a shitty plan, but walking toward the danger was better than running away.

"Are you going to knock?" Captain Nude-man asked.

I raised my hand to the wood then pulled it back. "I am. I mean, I think I am."

"We can do this tomorrow," he offered kindly. "No reason to do it now. Let's go home and dance some more."

"You know," I said, feeling light-headed and jittery, "that might be a good idea. I didn't really prep for this. Might help if I write a little script. Dick is pretty freaking scary."

"Works for me," Uncle Joe replied.

"Great." My sigh of relief was enormous.

The door to Dick's house opened. The man in question had opened it.

My horror-movie-worthy scream was unintentional... and wildly embarrassing.

"WHAT?" Uncle Joe shouted.

Quickly tapping the back of my coat so Captain Nude-man would pipe down, I plastered a smile on my face. It felt incredibly fake, but it was the best I had. "Dick. Oh my gosh! What a surprise!"

I wanted to kick my own ass. The line sucked. I sounded like an idiot.

The Demon squinted at me and stood in the open doorway of his home. I hadn't knocked. Had he felt my presence? Did Demons have Spidey-senses? Sadly, he looked ridiculously gorgeous—faded jeans that sat low on his hips and a sapphire-blue t-shirt... that matched his contact lenses. Bingo. If I could quit sticking my foot into my mouth and yanking it out of my butt, we could figure out if Dick could see Uncle Joe.

Dick's brow arched and he crossed his stupidly muscled arms over his broad chest. "It's a surprise that I'm at my house?"

"Well, kind of," I said, shoving him out of the way and walking in. "I would think since you bought a movie studio that you would be there working."

His expression was blank. For a hot sec I thought I saw bemusement, but he shut that right down. "My job is you," he said in a flat tone. "If you're at the studio, that's where I'll be."

"Got it," I said, taking a seat on the leather couch.

Dick was silent. He simply watched me and waited. It was unnerving. It made me more edgy than I already was. Speak. I needed to speak.

"So, how have you been doing?" I asked, then visibly winced.

I should not have spoken.

"Is that why you're here?" he inquired smoothly. "To find out how I'm doing?"

"Umm… no," I said. "My bad. I don't actually care how you're doing."

He laughed. I died a little inside. God, if I could dig the hole any deeper, I'd be buried. The Demon made me tongue-tied.

"Actually, I was thinking maybe we should get to know each other a little better," I blurted out, then immediately regretted my words. It sounded like a pick-up line. His smile was positively feral. It was so hot, I was sure my panties melted a little. However, he'd misunderstood in a big fat way.

Shit.

Closing my eyes, I pressed the bridge of my nose and groaned. "That came out all wrong."

"Your loss," he replied coolly.

I rolled my eyes. Dick was incredibly full of himself. It was also disgusting that he would even entertain the thought while banging Lilith. Making this operation stealthy and quick was the way to go. Being alone with Dick wasn't prudent. The less I said, the better off everyone was.

"Would you like something to drink?" he offered.

He had good manners for a Demon. I almost said I'd take a double shot of bourbon, but decided against it. Being tipsy would not behoove me. It might dull the nervousness, but it would also dull my inhibitions. Dick was too pretty to be around when I wasn't in full control.

"No, thank you. I'd like to discuss *Ass The World Turns*," I said.

"Wait," Uncle Joe shouted frantically from underneath my coat. "Was that the code word?"

Answering him wasn't really an option. But I could make it work. I was an actress and quick on my feet. "Yes! I would love to talk about *Ass The World Turns*."

Dick's expression was perplexed. I didn't blame him. I sounded insane.

"Here I come!" Uncle Joe announced. "Captain Nude-man at your service."

My dead uncle flew right out of my coat and seated himself next to me on the couch. My eyes were trained on Dick. He didn't seem to notice that a wrinkled gray dead person was sitting to my left. His gaze held mine.

"What do you want to discuss?" Dick inquired, still focused on me.

"I don't think Dick sees me," Uncle Joe whispered.

I didn't acknowledge Captain Nude-man, but I agreed. It would be incredibly difficult not to see a naked cadaver sitting on one's sofa. Dick had no reaction whatsoever.

"I have a cast list for the show," I said. "Do you want to approve it?"

"I don't," the Demon replied, sounding bored. "That's your gig, not mine."

I nodded, unsure what else to talk about. It was every kind of awkward.

"Wow! Dick is a very sexy man," Uncle Joe commented. "There is incredible sexual tension in the room, Cecily. Maybe you should fornicate with Dick. Just a thought."

I was thrilled beyond belief that Dick was not aware of the bullshit pouring from my uncle's mouth. It would be mortifying.

"So," I said, trying my damnedest not to yell at Captain Nude-man. "I think we can be ready to shoot in two weeks. Mariah is on top of everything and we have offers out."

"Again," Dick repeated. "Not my gig."

"Right," I said, realizing I was sweating. A coat in LA on an eighty-degree day was not necessary. However, when you were transporting a ghost, you did what you had to do.

"I believe I'll have a look around and see what Dick is hiding," Uncle Joe said, floating in the air above me. "My guess is that he's kinky. Dick looks like a tantric sex kind of fellow. And I'd put money on the fact that he's wild in the sack. I'll look for sex toys and furry handcuffs while I ascertain if he's out to kill you."

Trying to school my expression of horror was freaking hard. Dick didn't even twitch, which meant he'd heard none of it.

Or did he?

"SHIT," I shouted. How could Captain Nude-man and I have been so stupid? Dick might not be able to see my uncle, but there was a very good chance he could hear him. It didn't seem like it, but if Dick really was a million years old, he probably had an excellent poker face. "I HAVE TO GO NOW."

Uncle Joe zipped back into the living room. "We're leaving?"

"YES. WE, I MEAN, I HAVE TO GO NOW," I shouted as Dick stared at me like I'd lost my marbles.

"I was right about the sex toys, Cecily," Uncle Joe announced. "Lots of massage oils as well. I think you really might want to consider taking the Demon on a test run. Looks like a very good time."

Dick walked over to the front door and opened it. "Stop by anytime, Cecily."

"Thanks, but no," I muttered as I sprinted out of his house.

I prayed to shit I didn't believe in that Captain Nude-man had followed. I didn't need him floating around Dick's house searching for vibrators. This was such a disaster I wasn't sure what to do. While it didn't appear that Dick had heard Uncle Joe, appearances were wildly deceiving. The worst part of all of it was that I was now horny. Unbelievable. Did I have zero self-respect?

Clearly, the answer to the question was yes. I had none. Being turned on by a Demon who hated me and was fornicating—Uncle Joe's term—with my mom made me every kind of pathetic and gross.

I needed a bath. After the bath, I needed a shower. After that I needed about an hour alone in my bedroom. I had my own sex toys and I was about to use them to tamp down the wild, stupid, naked and incredibly naughty thoughts in my mind.

"Note for the future," I said as I arrived on my front porch breathing hard. "If a plan seems shitty, it's shitty."

"I thought we did a fine job," Uncle Joe protested, floating next to me.

"Duuuuude," I said, banging my forehead against the door on purpose. "We didn't think that through. While he couldn't see you, he could probably hear you."

There was a long moment of silence as Captain Nude-man and I just stared at each other.

"Oh my," Uncle Joe lamented. "I said some rather inappropriate things."

"You think?" I asked.

"I am so sorry, Cecily," he apologized. "Do you truly think he heard me?"

I shook my head and led us back into the house. Of course, Uncle Joe could have floated right through the wall, but I could not. "While it didn't seem like it, I have no clue. My guess would be yes. My fondest life's wish would be no."

"I have failed you," Uncle Joe said, near tears. "I don't deserve the superhero title of Captain Nude-man."

Flopping down on the couch, I sighed dramatically. "You didn't fail me. I'm one hundred percent at fault here. I forgot that I could hear you before I could see you. It's all on me. I missed a huge plot point."

"Absolutely not," Uncle Joe insisted, sitting down next to me on the couch. "I am to blame as well."

I mulled over the giant FUBAR and racked my brain for clues as to whether or not Dick had heard Uncle Joe. I honestly didn't know.

"Can I say something?" Uncle Joe asked.

I looked at him. He looked all kinds of naughty and a little smile pulled at his gray lips. "Not sure I want to hear it, but go for it."

"Dick wants you. Pretty sure I detected an erection," my

uncle said. "And no wonder! You're a stunningly beautiful woman."

"With incredibly shitty taste in men," I added, not touching the erection comment. "I find Dick attractive, but he's off limits. I won't fornicate with a Demon who's banging my mom."

Uncle Joe gasped. "Oh my! Does Bill know this?"

I shook my head. "He does not, and there's no reason to tell him. Ever."

"Yes. Yes, of course," he agreed. "It's only normal for someone to move on after forty years. Even Bill moved on with Sean's mom. Don't think he loved her like he loved Lilith, but he did love her."

I was getting a headache and I still needed to shower and enjoy a little date with my battery-operated-boyfriend, BOB.

"I'm going to take a quick nap then get back to work on the show," I said, standing up. "This day has kind of worn me out."

"Yes, dear. That is an excellent plan," Uncle Joe said. "I'll find something to do to keep me busy. Have you checked the expiration dates on the food in your refrigerator lately?"

I laughed. "Nope. Have at it, Captain Nude-man."

Uncle Joe zipped into the kitchen and right into the fridge.

Life was so very strange. And I had a feeling it would only keep getting stranger.

CHAPTER THIRTEEN

The day had been rough, but the evening was rocking.

Deciding it was safer to work from home than at the studio, I enlisted Sean and Man-mom to help me rearrange the furniture in my living room and turn it into a temporary working office space. Uncle Joe had supervised. My dad's visceral and vocal relief that I was going to hold meetings and auditions where the area was magically warded would have been funny if life wasn't so scary.

Mariah thought the idea was terrific, even though she had no clue as to the reason behind it. She said it gave the show a real family feel. The tiny ball-buster had also changed her name to Cher. My nutty agent volunteered to man the studio offices and deal with the technical side. I would deal with the creative from home for the next few days. Next week we'd all be at the studio.

The arrangement gave me the luxury of feeling safe and several days to get a head start on my Demon training with Dick. I seriously hoped I was a good student and could find my purple fire sword posthaste. Learning to defend myself was at the top of the list. I'd texted Dick to let him know I wanted to start in the morning at my house. I didn't trust myself to walk back over and ask. My earlier visit had taught me a fine and mortifying lesson. Thankfully, Man-mom had his number. I'd tossed his calling card back at him the day he'd taken me to Hell.

"Okay," Sean said with satisfaction after we'd met with the writers. "That was productive." He was pensive for a long beat. "I'd like to make you an offer, Cecily."

I held my breath and waited. I was just about to make my brother an offer. I'd planned to beg on my knees if I had to. The writers had just spent the better part of the evening with us at my bungalow. My choices had been brilliant. Of course, it helped that we were paying the big bucks. Rick Gee, Georgia Nagel, Kristen Calvert and Jameson Kall were some of the funniest people in Tinseltown. Sitting in the same room with them was an honor and a delight. Keeping up with them was dizzying. I hadn't laughed so hard in ages. They'd grilled me about the plot outlines, the characters and my vision, and then added their own hysterical two cents.

However, the King of The Comedy Evening was Sean Bloom.

My brother was a genius. Rick almost peed himself over the full-season story arc Sean had come up with. Jameson was giddy. Kristen jotted notes like her pants were on fire and Georgia was on the same page. After the meeting was over, Sean passed out baggies of jazz cabbage brownies to the gang. I was kind of appalled, but everyone was down with it.

"Your offer?" I asked my brother, trying to sound casual but failing miserably.

He grinned. "I'd like to be the head writer on *Ass The World Turns*. Thoughts?"

I screamed. Intelligible words wouldn't come out. I sounded like an alien.

Sean handed me an orange gummy. I swallowed it whole. "Is that a yes?"

I finally got hold of myself after a few more minutes of babbling. "It's the biggest yes in the Universe. I was ready to beg. You'll get a big fat paycheck for it."

My brother shrugged. "Not worried about that. Just give me what everyone else is getting. I think it'll be fun. And Georgia is hot."

"Umm... do not bang one of my writers," I warned my brother. "That'll end in a lawsuit."

Sean grinned. "Not to worry. Georgia and I have had a friends-with-benefits thing going on for two years," he informed me. "I've always wanted to work with her—she's funny as hell."

"Banging won't get in the way?" I asked, concerned.

"Banging makes it better," he assured me.

I wasn't as sure, but they were both adults and if the relationship was prior and mutual, then it was none of my business. Plus, Georgia was the first woman my brother had shown interest in who was his equal in so many ways. No wonder he'd ignored all the women swiping right on his Tinder app. Georgia was smart, lovely and hilarious. The thought of my brother finding something real delighted me, but I didn't pry. I wanted to, but I didn't. However, I'd watch that situation unfold like a hawk. Maybe one of us would finally get it right in the romance department.

"Fine," I said, giving him a hug. "We could blow this baby out of the water."

"Not could. Will," he replied, resting his forehead against mine. "Still concerns me that you'll be so front and center, but no one could do it but you. You were made for this. It's your time, sis."

My terror was severalfold. Sucking on the show would suck. With the writers, crew and cast, that would be pretty hard to do. Dying would suck. Getting offed by flaming assholes wasn't in my control, but learning to defend myself was in my control.

"I start training with Dick in the morning," I said.

"Where?" Sean asked.

"Here. The backyard."

He nodded. "Time?"

I checked my phone to see if Dick the Demon had texted back. He had. I made a face. "Sunup."

"Little early for me, but I'll be here," Sean promised, standing up to leave. "I'm sure Man-mom will want to be here too."

"And I will be here as well," Uncle Joe announced, flying into the room.

I took out my contact lens so I could see him. "Captain Nude-man," I said with a wave. "You can't talk when Dick is around, just in case he can hear you. We made enough of a mess earlier."

"True that!" he agreed.

"Is there a story there?" Sean asked, pausing at the front door on his way out.

"Yes, and I'm not telling it," I replied. "Some things are better left a humiliating mystery."

"Been there, done that," Sean said with a salute as he left for the evening.

Uncle Joe was a little frantic. He floated around the room like a drunk on a bender. All I wanted to do was get a good night's sleep before getting my butt handed to me in the morning, but it was abundantly clear that Uncle Joe wanted to talk.

"Fifteen minutes," I said, sitting back down on the couch. "Then I have to go to bed."

"Cecily, I found some things out," he said. "I went spying at Dick's house while you had your meetings—I stayed silent the entire time."

My gut tightened. Uncle Joe's demeanor didn't bode well for a pleasant chat. "Tell me."

"Don't fornicate with him," he advised. "Two unsavory women stopped by."

"Eww," I gagged out. "He had a threesome?"

"No, no," Uncle Joe said. "Didn't fornicate with either one of them. However, he seemed to be acquainted with them *very* well, if you know what I mean. They arrived and left separately, but I didn't like the looks of them."

"Were they Demons?" Dick had promised the area was magically warded, but now I wasn't so sure he'd been truthful. However, if they were Demons, they could be on Team Lilith.

"Not a clue," he admitted. "Blonde hussies. He promised each a contract on your show. It sounded like one might have already been hired."

"What?" I hissed. The jerk had given me full creative control. He didn't even watch TV. Now he thought he was inserting blonde Demon hookers into the cast?

Not happening.

Dick was a dick. He might have a purple fire sword, but I had an ironclad contract. One might think Demons were scary, but they'd never met a showbiz entertainment lawyer.

"Yes," Uncle Joe said, wringing his hands. "I was hidden under the couch, so I missed quite a bit of the conversations. Didn't want to risk being seen."

"Was Dick wearing contacts?"

"No," Uncle Joe said. "That's why I hid."

"Is he trying to kill me?"

Uncle Joe pressed his papery lips together and fretted. "I'm not sure. Your name came up several times, but I couldn't make out what was being said—lots of arguing. Dick has dust bunnies under his couch. It was all I could do to keep from sneezing."

"Wait," I said, confused. "You're dead."

"Correct."

"And you don't have bodily functions," I reminded him.

"Accurate."

"But you still have allergies to dust bunnies?" I asked, squinting at him.

Uncle Joe's mouth fell open. "Well, I'll be! Do you think it was psycho symptomatic?"

"I don't know," I said, getting down on my hands and knees and looking under my couch for a dust bunny. No dust bunnies. Normally that would thrill me. Today, not as much. I wanted to test the theory.

"Maybe I'm not as dead as I thought," he mused as he continued to dart around the living room.

I didn't know how to respond to that one, so I didn't. Uncle Joe was definitely dead. "Can you describe the women? Ages? Names?"

"Didn't get names," he said, finally settling himself on the armchair. "Large breasts—very large."

"Of course," I said with a grunt of disgust. "Dick is obviously a *beewb* guy."

"Sadly, it seems to be the case," Uncle Joe agreed. "Best not to fornicate with a man-whore."

I nodded absently. The evil green-eyed monster dancing in

my mind pissed me off. Why I felt jealousy was absurd. I was not dating Dick. I would never date Dick. I didn't like Dick. He was a disgusting man who happened to be the hottest jerk I'd ever seen. Not only was he doing the deed with my mom, he apparently had a roster of *beewby* bimbos on the side. What did I expect? He was a kagillion-year-old Demon.

"Describe them, please." There were hundreds of busty blondes in LA. The chances of me knowing them were slim. "Ages?"

"That's the unusual part," Uncle Joe said with a perplexed expression. "When they arrived, I would have sworn early twenties. But during the course of their visits, they aged."

"What do you mean?"

My uncle scratched his head. I was glad it wasn't his balls. "There were terse conversations. At points I would swear they were speaking in a foreign language, but the dust bunnies messed with my spying skills. I must do some reading about phantom symptoms after death. Such a surprising conundrum. However, if there's a way to regain bodily functions, I would love to be able to have a nice BM again."

We had veered way off course. "Umm… okay. How about we get back to the aging thing?"

"So sorry," Uncle Joe said contritely. "But I do miss a good BM."

"Understandable," I replied, not wanting to make him feel bad.

"As I said, when they each arrived, they were young. When they left, the first one was in her sixties and the other around forty."

I mulled that over. It was possible Uncle Joe was mistaken. He'd been hiding under a couch with dust bunnies. Or he was correct and Demons could control their ages. It made sense. Dick didn't look a day over forty-five.

"Are you going to bring it up with Abaddon tomorrow?" Uncle Joe inquired.

"Can't," I told him. "There is no way I know this information. It would blow your cover. And his name is Dick, not Abaddon."

"Excellent point," he agreed. "Also, I believe you got his name incorrect or he gave you an alias. The voluptuous blondes called him Abaddon."

Dick had told me his name was Abaddon—Abe to his friends. The large-knockered gals were not his friends. Honestly, I'd be shocked if he had any friends. He was an asshole.

"His name is Abaddon," I said. "I renamed him Dick for obvious reasons."

"His penis size?" my uncle asked.

I almost choked on my own spit. "Absolutely not," I snapped. "I haven't seen his penis and have no plans to see it. I named him Dick because of his attitude."

"Of course," Uncle Joe said. "My mistake."

I blew out an audible puff of air. It was a good time to end the conversation. I was now imagining what Dick's privates looked like.

"Thank you, Captain Nude-man."

He smiled and patted my head. His hand went right through me, but the thought counted. "I'm so sorry the information isn't good."

"Remains to be seen," I said, standing up. "Right now, it's simply information—not good, not bad. We're in the gathering stage. Anything we can find out is to our benefit. The more we learn the better armed we are."

"You would have been a wonderful spy," he said.

"Played one in a mini-series about a decade ago," I said with a laugh. I'd have to pull out the script from the show. I kept all my old scripts for sentimental reasons. There were boxes of them in the garage.

"And now you're playing one in real life!" Uncle Joe announced with pride.

I'd rather just be playing myself in real life. The extra roles were enough to schedule double therapy appointments. However, none of what was going on in my life right now could be discussed in therapy. I'd just have to get it all out with the three people I trusted the most—Man-mom, Sean and Captain Nude-man.

"And on that disturbing revelation, I'm going to bed."

"Get some sleep," Uncle Joe advised. "And tomorrow after the training session, we must go to the grocery. You have vegetables growing hair in the fridge."

I winced. "Seriously?"

"Yes, but not to worry. I've made a list and we can get you set up! Must stay healthy, Cecily. I have a feeling you will need to be in top form. Change is coming."

Change is coming. The words were prophetic. Not all change was bad. The changes so far had not been expected or wanted —other than the TV show and the arrival of Uncle Joe. But I was an actress. Pretending was my forte. I just hoped I could pretend my way into living a few more decades.

I had a lot going on and no time to die.

CHAPTER FOURTEEN

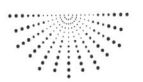

"Holy hell," I muttered, peeking through the bottom corner of the blinds into the backyard. "That's just not right."

I was squatting and hiding in my kitchen. It was ridiculous. But what was more ridiculous was that Dick had arrived early and was warming up to either teach me or kill me. That was to be expected. What I hadn't expected was that the Demon would be barely clothed.

All he wore were thin gray sweatpants. Nothing else. His body was a freaking work of art—streamlined and muscular. I wasn't sure how I was going to concentrate and avoid dying if I had to look at him.

"Shit," I whispered. "I think he did that on purpose. If he accidentally kills me because I'm distracted, then it's not his fault. Evil."

"Two can play that game," Uncle Joe said, scaring the heck out of me.

True to form, I screamed. My scream startled Captain Nude-man, so he screamed. I blanched as I watched Dick roll his eyes then glance over at the window with an arched brow. I was beyond uncool. I'd probably just lost a lot of Demon points.

Quickly ducking, I slid down the wall and sat on the floor. There was no way he didn't hear me. The question was, did he hear my uncle?

"Well, that was certainly an interesting way to start the day," Uncle Joe commented. "Felt kind of cathartic!"

"More like embarrassing," I corrected him, crawling over to the counter and grabbing a banana. The blinds were closed, but I wasn't taking any chances of being spotted again. I was still in my PJs.

"Honest reactions should not be shameful," he said. "No legacy is so rich as honesty."

"William Shakespeare," I said immediately.

"Correct," Uncle Joe replied. "How about this one? Honesty is the first chapter in the book of wisdom."

"Thomas Jefferson."

"Yes! Far easier to be truthful. Lies are tremendously difficult to remember, Cecily," he explained. "It's a waste of precious time to live a lie."

I peeled the banana and considered my uncle's words. "But I have been—living a lie, that is. I've been a Demon my whole life and living as a human."

"I disagree," Uncle Joe said. "You've only just discovered your other side and you *are* human—at least half."

I took a bite, chewed slowly and swallowed. "This conversation is bizarre."

He chuckled. "No more bizarre than having it with your dead relative."

He had a point. "What did you mean two could play that game?"

Captain Nude-man giggled. "Go out there in a bathing suit. My guess is that Dick's eyes would pop out of his head."

I groaned. "Not what we're going for. I need the Demon to train me. Learning to use the purple fire sword and getting Dick out of my life is the end goal. Displaying my girls won't be helpful."

Uncle Joe nodded. "You're right, dear niece. I just thought giving the man a taste of his own medicine would be a nice metaphorical kick in the gonads. If he wants to play games, then you should win, not him."

"I want to win," I muttered, flipping on the switch to the coffee maker while still staying low. "But I would bet good money the Demon plays dirty."

"Possibly," he agreed. "Why not look at this as an acting role? Your character is a newly minted Demon who is dealing with an adversary who may or may not have her best interests at heart. The episode is to extract information from your opponent so he cannot get the upper hand."

"Holy cow," I said, looking at my uncle in a new light. Maybe I should hire him to write for *Ass The World Turns*. "Keep going. It's terrific."

Uncle Joe clasped his transparent hands together and grinned with delight. "Do you know anything about Demons?"

I shook my head. "Other than they have weird eyes, a violent streak and purple fire swords, no."

"That's where you shall start," he replied. "Avoid combat until you understand your weapons. You cannot fight blind. It's a losing proposition."

"Okay," I said, crawling out of the kitchen and toward my bedroom to get dressed as Uncle Joe floated beside me. "First episode is fact finding."

"Yes! Keep your enemy off balance. Let him get sloppy. He's liable to reveal more if you throw him off his game."

"It pisses him off when I call him Dick," I said as I dug through the clean laundry that I hadn't folded yet.

"Then throw in a few Abaddons to surprise him."

"Good plan. Today I'll learn my history. Tomorrow I will use it to live my future."

"Who coined that quote?" Uncle Joe asked, perplexed. "It's fabulous."

"Me. I coined it," I replied, shooing him out of my bedroom so I could get dressed.

"Wonderful!" he sang as he floated away. "Brilliant and beautiful."

I wasn't sure I agreed with his assessment, but would take the compliment happily. Looking down at the clothing in my hands, I grinned. Yes, I would wear something comfortable and respectable. However, in every good plot there was a twist. There was a fine chance I wouldn't be able to pull the twist off, but like any actress worth her salt... I was going to be prepared.

∽

The sun had risen. The California heat came along for the ride. A blazing orange glow lit my backyard and bounced off the lemon trees and red bougainvillea. It gave the backyard a sultry feel. The half-naked Demon fit right in.

The air was thick with something unfamiliar. It was heavy on my skin and made it a little difficult to breathe. My guess yesterday would have been smog. Today my guess was magic... powerful and deadly magic belonging to my Demon protector who didn't like me.

Why I found that sexy was infuriating.

Inhaling as deeply as I could, I reminded myself sternly that I had a bounty on my head and was in danger of biting the big one at any moment. Yep, Abaddon was a beautiful being, but looks meant nothing if the insides were rotten. The Demon was a means to an end to learn how to stay alive. While I didn't trust him as far as I could throw him—which would not be far at all—I would approach the lesson with an open mind. I had a whole lot to lose if I didn't understand how to defend myself.

"You're late," he snapped.

I hadn't worn my contact lens. He hadn't worn his either. His silver pupils sparkled as his gaze landed on mine. It was stupidly hot. If this was a movie, it's where he would have approached me, taken me into his arms and kissed me senseless.

It was not a movie and if he tried to kiss me, I'd knee his nuts into his esophagus. Not to mention, it was dumb to think he would want to kiss me. He already had his plate full with gal pals, including the woman who had given birth to me. I'd play that splash of icy-cold water through my head when I found him appealing. It was a lady-boner killer.

"Sun's still rising," I said curtly. "You didn't specify a time, Dick."

"You're rude," he shot back, annoyed.

"Apparently, I'm a Demon. Sue me."

I was pretty sure his lip quirked in the corner. "You asked for the lesson—which is comical. If you can't be bothered to be on time, which means *early*, I won't grace you with this opportunity again, Cecily."

"Ego much?" I snapped.

"Pain in my ass," he muttered.

"To make an insult land, you have to throw it at someone

who cares. I don't," I said flatly. "It's *not comical* that I want to learn to defend myself. You don't want the bodyguard job and I don't want you here."

"You know nothing about me or what I want," he said coldly. "You're a child. Nothing could prepare you to defeat the ones who want you dead."

I rolled my eyes. "Awesome. I'm forty—hardly a child—and I call bullshit. Just like I don't know you, you do not know me, Abaddon."

He shrugged and his eyes narrowed. "Did you just call me by my name?"

"I did."

"Interesting."

"Not really," I said in a bored tone.

He waited for me to say more. I didn't.

"Fine. Hit me. Let's see what you've got," he challenged.

I squinted at him like he'd grown another head. I'd watched him decapitate flaming assholes. I wasn't about to land a punch that could possibly be reciprocated. I was not an idiot. As Uncle Joe had very wisely pointed out, I needed to know what was in my arsenal before I used it. "No thanks. Today I want to understand my history. Why is it a problem that I'm my mother's daughter? What's the name of the whackadoo goddess who wants me six feet under? Do I have Demon powers innately? Why were you sent to protect me if you hate my guts?" I was on a roll. "Are there other Demons in LA? Are they on Team Lilith? If so, can one of them protect me instead of you?"

His full lips compressed to a tight thin line. "You done?"

"Just getting started," I shot back. "Why should I trust you?"

"You shouldn't," he replied.

His eyes began to glow and a shimmering red mist danced and weaved through the backyard. I didn't take that as a great sign. Glancing around, I looked for Man-mom and Sean. They must have overslept. Pretty sure I was in way over my head, I wondered if I should take a potty break and call them.

Running away to the wilds of Colorado was starting to sound like a decent plan.

Nope. Not running. At least not yet. Right now, I would stand my ground in the relative safety of my backyard and get some answers. Dick thought I was a pain in the ass. Fine. I would make that come true and then some.

"For all I know, you gave me the TV show so it would be easier for the bad guys to find me. It's a very convenient theory. My blood wouldn't be on your hands. I'm dead and your precious Lilith can't blame her boy-toy. Win-win."

"Fucking nightmare," he hissed as he paced the backyard like a caged tiger.

"The worst kind," I agreed with him. "Have you figured out who told on me? And to that point, is the bounty on my head going to last for the rest of my life?"

Abaddon snapped his fingers and a cushioned lawn chair appeared. *One* cushioned lawn chair. He sat down on it and glared at me.

It was a nifty trick. If I couldn't find my purple fire sword, maybe I could conjure up furniture and trip all of my enemies.

Marching over to my patio, I dragged a chair over and placed it in front of the jackass. "Answer my questions," I demanded as I sat down and crossed my arms over my chest.

"You don't give up," he commented, eyeing me with annoyance.

"Our greatest weakness lies in giving up. The most certain way to succeed is always to try just one more time."

"Thomas Edison," Abaddon said with a tight smile and a shake of his head.

I was impressed.

"Look, Dick," I said, keeping my eyes on his face so they didn't stray and get stuck on his abs. "I don't know what you normally do as a Demon. I'm sure having to protect a half-human, half-Demon wasn't in the plan. It certainly wasn't in mine. So, I'm sorry that you have to do this. All I want is to learn some ways to stay alive. You're not with me twenty-four-seven. And soon you'll probably get a new assignment or job or whatever they call it in Hell. We don't have to like each other. We just have to get along for a little while. Chances are good I'm going to get decapitated soon anyway. I really want to give the flaming asshole who chops my head off a run for his money and not die like a wimp. Can you understand that?"

"Hell is a misnomer," he replied. "It's called the Darkness."

I nodded. I wasn't sure why that was important, but I was listening. "My questions?"

He rested his head on the back of the chair and stared at the sky.

It was hot.

I immediately pictured him banging my mom—who I'd actually never seen, but it did the trick. Lady-boner dead.

Abaddon inhaled then exhaled like I'd asked him to go shopping with me and hold my purse. "Fine. Number one, it disrupts the power balance and brings the prophecy to light. Number two, Pandora. Number three, innate. Number four, I chose to willingly. Number five, Yes. Number six, some. Number seven, absolutely not. Number eight, already answered. Number nine, no. Number ten, yes."

My mouth formed a perfect O. The Demon had just done as I'd asked and bested me. I had no clue what the answers to any of my questions were. I had no clue in what order I'd asked them. Dammit. If I'd made a script, I could have figured it out.

I didn't even think to bring a freaking notebook or a pencil. The only things that popped out and made sense were that the mean goddess's name was Pandora and that there was some kind of prophecy that had landed me in hot water.

There was nothing to do but laugh or cry. I opted for laughing. "Alrighty then, that was wildly unhelpful."

The Demon smiled. It was stunning. "You ask and you shall receive, Cecily."

"Good to know. I want a purple fire sword," I said.

Abaddon sighed dramatically. He stared at me long and hard. I didn't look away. Considering it was terrifying, I was proud of myself.

"You have one," he finally said.

"Where is it?"

"Inside you."

I looked down at myself and groaned. "This is one of those bullshit 'if you build it, they will come' moments," I muttered.

"I have no clue what you're referring to, but you have to will it," he replied. "It's not easy."

I held up my hand. "But it's also not impossible."

"No. It's not impossible," he conceded.

"Show me. Please."

Abaddon reached out and took my hand in his. A tingle shot through my body at his touch. It felt magical and right. I didn't blink an eye. Neither did he. Maybe he didn't feel it. Maybe it was normal for Demons. It wasn't normal for me.

"Wait," I said, deciding that embarrassment didn't matter. I'd just partaken in a conversation with my dead uncle about honesty. I may as well go that route. "Did you feel that?"

"Feel what?"

I felt my cheeks heat, but kept going. "That tingle... when we touched."

"No. I felt nothing." His face was expressionless.

His pause before he spoke was a fraction of a hair too long for a human, but I reminded myself quickly that he was not human. I mentally reprimanded myself for being an idiot. I was a sucker for a bad guy. Abaddon wasn't on the market. I was pretty sure he'd just lied, but it furthered my argument that I needed to date my battery-operated-boyfriend and stop having naughty thoughts about a dude from Hell.

Done. I was going to shut that door in my head and lock it. It was appalling that I kept thinking about the Demon in a sexual way. My freaking life was on the line. I didn't need to get laid by my mother's lover. I needed to live.

"Great!" I said a little louder than intended. "Let's do it."

"Close your eyes, Cecily," he instructed.

"Shit, are we going back to Hell?" The last time he'd told me to close my eyes it had resulted in a heinous acid trip.

"The Darkness," he corrected me. "And no. It's not safe for you to go back."

"Got it. One more question before I conjure up a flaming asshole-killing light saber."

Abaddon sucked his bottom lip into his mouth and stared at me. I wasn't sure if he was trying not to laugh or let me have it.

"What is the prophecy that's causing all the trouble?"

"Trouble is a rather mild word," he said.

"Semantics," I replied.

This time he did smile. I felt a sense of victory that the meanie smiled. Most often in his eyes I saw pain or anger. It was none of my business, but it was there.

"The Demon Goddess who comes from two worlds shall bring on the end."

I let that sink in. "Seriously?"

"Yes."

"Well, that's stupid," I snapped.

The Demon's brows shot up.

"The end of what? The world? The day? The meal? The bullshit? I mean, for the love of everything vague, that's the reason the flaming assholes want my head?" I released his hand then threw mine in the air. "I cannot believe I might have died the other day because a bunch of idiots are following what basically amounts to a vague sentence. Do you see how absurd this is, Dick?"

Dick was speechless. He just sat there with his mouth agape.

"I call so much bullshit," I yelled. "You would think that randomly killing someone without any solid evidence would be illegal. But of course, we're talking about Demons. Is everyone stupid down there, or what?"

The Demon's mouth compressed. Dick was pissed. I didn't care. He might not want to talk, but I sure did.

"I didn't ask for Lilith to be my mother. I didn't ask to be a Demon. I had no choice in this shitshow." I laughed. An ugly puzzle piece snapped together. "And yes, I'm onto why you hate me so much. It must be horrifying to have to protect the daughter of the woman you're fornicating with—especially since she apparently loved my dad. How demoralizing."

Abaddon's eyes were now shooting silver sparks. I was probably minutes away from losing my head. Whatever. I was bummed I wouldn't get to do the show. I'd miss Man-mom and Sean like crazy, but if Uncle Joe could stick around, maybe I could too. It would suck not to eat, but I'd be cool with not having my period anymore.

If my end was inevitable, then I was going out at full-volume. The cat-and-mouse crap was not working for me.

"Did you just imply that I'm having sex with my Goddess?" Abaddon snarled.

I rolled my eyes. "I implied nothing, asshole. I said it."

The Demon walked over to my favorite lemon tree and waved his hand. The beautiful tree hissed and sizzled then turned to ash before my eyes.

"You did not just obliterate my lemon tree," I shouted.

"It was better than you," he shouted back.

That tree wasn't cheap and I'd babied it for years. I didn't have kids. I didn't have a dog. I didn't even have a cat. I had my trees. Dick had just killed the closest thing I had to a child.

A rage boiled up inside of me I didn't know I possessed. I had to admit it was a little overkill, considering it was polite of Dick to have incinerated a tree instead of me. However, it wasn't just the tree. There was an exploding laundry list of shit that began to swirl in my furious mind.

I was a hunted woman due to the heinous female Demon who had given birth to me and then left. It would have been kinder to have never had me. Lilith couldn't have loved my dad. If she had truly loved him, she would have never put him in mortal danger.

She was a Demon in every sense of the word. I hated her.

I would be looking over my shoulder for the rest of my life.

Trusting Abaddon was a risk. My gut told me it was fine, but my gut had also told me that doing an informercial for hair loss was fine. That had backfired. The rags reported I was bald for years.

But the worst of all of it was that my dad and my brother were in danger because of me. That was not acceptable.

The tingling started in my toes and quickly spread through my body. No one was going to harm the people I loved.

No one.

The sparks of fire that shot from my fingertips as I imagined the flaming assholes decapitating Sean shocked me. But it also felt oh so right.

Slashing my hands through the air, I set the lawn chair Dick had conjured up on fire. It was glorious. The flames began to spread. I wiggled my fingers and helped them along. The power was intoxicating.

With a clap of his hands, Abaddon vanquished my beautiful fires. Didn't matter. I simply started more.

The ringing in my ears was loud, but there was a rhythm to it. The drum beat was sensual and animalistic. I went with it. The plot twist was happening. It was not the one I'd planned. I figured I'd reveal the bikini I was wearing under my sweats. But nope, this was so much better.

Closing my eyes, I raised my hands to the sky. The searing heat that suffused my body made me think I might be pulling fire from the sun. My hair whipped my face and I'd never felt more alive. It was good to be me.

My laugh sounded distant and unhinged, but when the purple fire sword arrived, I felt it. My entire arm vibrated and the power I felt was overwhelming. Maybe I'd lop off Abaddon's head before he lopped off mine.

"Son of a bitch," Abaddon roared.

"Holy shit!" Sean cried out.

"What have you done to her?" Man-mom bellowed, clearly frantic.

"I burned her tree down," Abaddon snarled. "I was unaware of her attachment."

"Dude," Sean said. "You really stepped in it."

The voices were far away, but I listened to the conversation.

"Cecily," Man-mom said.

My eyes opened and I watched my dad approach me through a bloody red mist. It was strange and pretty. Man-mom was such a beautiful and good man.

"Do not go to her," Abaddon snapped.

"Screw you," Sean shouted as he joined my dad.

"It's okay, baby," Man-mom said soothingly as he slowly made his way toward me. "It's me. I won't hurt you. Put the fires out."

"Back away," Abaddon warned again. "She's not in control. Cecily, you could kill them."

His words were like ice shooting through my veins. The Demon was correct. I backed away from my dad and brother. The flames around me increased. My goal was to protect my family, not murder them. Turning to the Demon who despised me, I reached out to him.

I was literally on fire now and small explosions occurred with every movement I made. I felt the golden flames lick my skin. There was no pain. My body enjoyed the inferno consuming me, but my mind knew it was wrong. The destruction I was causing made me want to cause more. The vicious cycle was going to end all of us.

"Help me," I begged in a whisper, locking my gaze on Abaddon's. "Make this stop. Please."

The Demon walked toward me with purpose. His gorgeous body shook with power. I struggled to breathe.

"Don't fight me, Cecily," he commanded.

"Am I going to die?" I asked as the flames turned a blinding silver and danced wildly over my skin.

"Not today."

Wrapping me in his arms and pulling my burning body against his, he began to chant in a language I didn't understand —the same one he'd spoken in his office. The melodic words calmed my soul, and I watched in fascination as his body absorbed the fiery magic that had controlled me.

Abaddon didn't flinch. He didn't make a sound. He stared into my eyes and straight into my soul.

The need to destroy stopped as abruptly as it had begun.

My purple fire sword was gone. The heat was gone. The feeling of absolute power was gone. One of the worst parts… all of my clothes were gone—even the bathing suit. I was naked and pressed against the man who'd been starring in my pornographic dreams.

Nothing about it was sexual. It made sense. I'd been on fire. I was shocked that I was alive.

The shame was intense—debilitating. I'd turned into a monster and I'd liked it.

"Here you go, baby," Man-mom said, wrapping my shaking body in the table cloth from the picnic table. "Let's take you inside."

I nodded. But before I walked away, I pulled Abaddon's head down and whispered in his ear. "Thank you, Abaddon. I need a favor."

"What is it?" His voice was tight and his eyes were wild.

I didn't know if he was furious or felt badly for me. It didn't matter.

"What is my status as a Demon?" I asked. "Am I a goddess? In the prophecy you said Demon Goddess."

His nod was curt. "You are."

"Does that trump your position?"

He squinted at me in distrust. "Why?"

"Answer me," I said.

"Yes," he ground out.

I smiled. There was no way I was going to live like this. I was a walking time bomb ready to explode. Abaddon might have helped me contain the power inside me for now, but I felt it bubbling under my skin begging to come back out to play. I had no doubt that my end was coming soon. There was no way in Hell—or the Darkness—that I was taking my dad and my brother with me. The solution was surprisingly simple.

"I need you to kill me."

His eyes narrowed to slits of fury. Man-mom and Sean hadn't heard a word. That was the way I wanted it. This was between me and Abaddon—Demon to Demon.

"No," he ground out.

"Yes," I shot back as I moved away and smiled at him. "Goddesses trump bodyguards."

Abaddon turned his back on me. It didn't matter. He had to do as I'd asked, and I knew he'd do the deed quickly and as painlessly as possible. Win-win.

It was the only way.

CHAPTER FIFTEEN

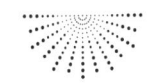

Having a meeting about the TV show was surreal considering I had been on fire only hours earlier. Shockingly, there was no evidence of the blaze. Not one bit. My backyard was pristine—even the lemon tree had been replaced. Uncle Joe had hidden and watched as Abaddon did some voodoo and righted all the wrongs I'd committed.

The most offensive wrong I'd committed was almost killing Man-mom and Sean, and that was why I'd set up my own demise. That would be discussed soon with Dick. Maybe we could get the show up and running before my death. I didn't actually need to be in it. The concept was so damned good that it would be an incredible showcase for any actress. As long as I created it, it would live on. That would have to be enough.

I'd found my purple fire sword and I no longer wanted it. If my enemies found out what I'd discovered, I was sure the bounty on my head would be increased exponentially. Rage had been the spark to ignite the flame. There had been no skill to calling on my power. It came freely when I felt an all-consuming fury. I wasn't even sure I could get there again unless Sean or Man-mom were in true danger. However, the strange feelings churning inside me made me think it might not be all that difficult to call back the fire.

"Hello, anybody home in there?" Jenni asked, waving her hand in front of my face.

"Oh my God," I said, yanking my mind into the present and the job at hand. "So sorry, I didn't get much sleep last night."

Jenni tilted her head and examined me. We were sitting on the floor in my living room with scads of headshots and makeup color palettes surrounding us.

I'd taken a long shower and an hour nap after the lesson that went to Hell—metaphorically speaking. Abaddon had left and let Man-mom know I was not to leave the area until further notice. Right now, I was fine with that. If I ran into a flaming asshole there was a fine chance I'd blow up the entire city of Los Angeles by accident.

I would not hide forever, but a few cooldown days were needed. Plus, I'd already set up the working from home angle for the week.

Jenni pursed her lips and absently braided the silver streak in her hair. "You look a little tired, Cecily. But I swear to Jesus in a jockstrap, you've lost ten years off your life. You look thirty. For real."

"Are you shitting me?" I asked, grabbing a mirror and peering into it. "What the fu..."

Jenni's face popped up behind me and joined mine in the reflection. "Botox?" she asked,

"Umm... no," I said.

"Filler?"

"Nope."

Jenni was stymied. "Great sex?"

I laughed. BOB had been good but I wouldn't say my battery-operated-boyfriend was great.

"Sadly, no," I told her with another laugh.

She shrugged and went back to work putting color palettes with headshots. "Whatever you're doing, keep doing it. You look incredible."

Not gonna happen. Lighting myself on fire was hopefully a one-time affair. It was shocking I wasn't scarred from head to toe. I stared at my face in the mirror. Jenni was correct. Gone were my grumpy grooves. Gone were all the fine lines on my face. Not that I was a huge hot mess before, but I'd been slowly showing the signs of aging. Now? Nada.

If I reverted back to my twenties, it would be a big problem. I was about to play a forty-year-old actress on the job of my dreams... maybe. I'd have to talk to Abaddon about it. Uncle Joe had said the hussies who'd visited Abaddon had changed their ages. If I had a purple fire sword, I would imagine I could control my age. If not, I was screwed.

"Oh, you have twelve blowtorches on your front porch," Jenni added.

My eyes grew wide and I almost laughed. "Interesting."

Jenni nodded. "My thought exactly. Anyhoo," Jenni said, looking at the lineup of the cast's headshots. "This is the Dream Team. All this talent on one show. Unheard of."

I grinned and pushed the events of the morning and the blowtorches to the back of my mind. Right now, it was time to work with one of my best friends.

"It's pretty awesome," I agreed. "Is Sushi coming over?"

Jenni shook her head and didn't make eye contact. "Don't think so. She said she was dealing with some shit and would check in later this afternoon."

"She okay?" I asked. Something was fishy.

Sushi was a blunt and all business kind of gal—very low drama along with her very low-cut shirts. I'd worked with her on too many gigs to count. It always amazed me how often we worked together. Luck, I suppose. She was amazing at her job. Her flair for fashion was insane.

Jenni leaned in close. "If I tell you something, can you keep it to yourself?"

If she only knew of all the *things* I was keeping to myself... "Absolutely."

"Sushi got a boob job. Today."

My eyes widened. "Shut the front door. Her boobs are fantastic. I mean, she's a babe for her age. Why in the heck would she do that?"

"Don't know," Jenni said. "And I don't think she likes the results."

"Did you see them?" I asked, grabbing a bag of chips, taking a few then handing the bag over.

She shook her head and put a chip in her mouth. "She texted before I came over and said she was pissed."

"Bizarre."

"And then some," Jenni agreed. "She's already a C cup. If she went to a D or an E, it's not going to be her best look."

I pictured Sushi with an E cup and sighed. I hated what women in Hollywood felt they had to do to stay relevant. Sushi wasn't even in front of the camera and had clearly felt the pressure. Poor little Rhoda, the nip slip gal from the soap audition, had definitely had some work done at twenty. And Ophelia... Lordy, the list was too long to name all the procedures that unpleasant woman had partaken in.

"Show business is harsh," I muttered.

"Drop the show and all you're left with is business," Jenni said, lying down on the floor.

Nodding, I added two more cents. "As Francis Ford Coppola said, whom God wishes to destroy, He first makes successful in show business."

"I'm more of a Richard Pryor kind of devotee," Jenni said with a grin. "I love show business. I wake up every morning and kiss it."

I laughed. "Does it kiss you back?"

"Most of the time," she said, rolling onto her stomach. "I guess I'm still young at heart even if I'm slightly older in the knees."

"You're fifty. That's the new forty," I reminded my buddy.

"That's right! However, lately I've noticed that I can forget what I'm doing while I'm doing it."

"Been there, done that," I told her, stealing back the bag of chips. "Sometimes I feel like my sanity is hanging out near my impending midlife crisis."

Jenni chuckled. "My motto is, don't let midlife get you down. It's too hard to get back up."

"You're a dork," I said.

"Till the end. You wanna get back to work? I figure since Sushi will probably be down for a bit, we can pick fabric swatches to go with the makeup color palettes. Save her some time. She can change anything she wants to, but we can get her started."

"How long does it take to recover from a boob job?"

Jenni shrugged. "Four to six weeks, but Sushi said she'll be up and running by the weekend."

I made a face. "Today is Friday. Tomorrow is the weekend. Not possible."

"It's Sushi. She's a bulldozer."

This wasn't good. There was no way I would let her go from the show, but I was going to make damned sure she had plenty of help. I didn't want her lifting anything. Quickly texting Cher, I gave her the go ahead to hire double the size of a normal costume crew. Cher texted back and said she was on it. She also informed me she was stopping by later this afternoon. Note to self… hide all incriminating objects. My agent was a snooper.

It would be pricey to double the crew, but Dick was paying the bills and Sushi was my friend—more like a longtime friendly acquaintance, but still. My cast, staff and crew were going to be treated royally. I still couldn't wrap my head around Sushi getting a boob job, but that was her business, not mine.

"Do you want to read the pilot?" I asked Jenni.

"Do you ask stupid questions?" she shot right back.

"Umm… probably." I grinned.

Jenni hopped up to her feet. Her knees were just fine. "You do," she assured me. "Of course, I want to read the pilot!"

"Sean delivered it not long before you got here. Still a work in progress. I just skimmed it and laughed my ass off," I explained, grabbing the paper copy Sean had given me.

All of the pages were watermarked. I couldn't believe how fast the writers had put it together. But the word was that my killer humiliating audition stories made it a breeze. I was glad my mortifying moments were finally going to pay off.

"Wine or soda?" Jenni asked, walking to the kitchen.

"Soda for me," I called out. Getting tipsy was not on the table right now. I needed my wits about me 24/7. I was multi-tasking like a fiend. Considering one of the tasks was staying alive, I figured I'd stay off the sauce for the foreseeable future. One never knew when one might run into a flaming asshole.

CHAPTER SIXTEEN

Jenni left after we'd read the pilot and laughed until our sides hurt. She was going to check on Sushi then set up her offices at the studio. She'd hired a terrific makeup and hair crew and needed to get the area ready.

It was good to have a dear friend like Jenni. Our history in the biz tied us together, but our friendship had endured because we adored and respected each other. Total win.

"How am I going to make all of this work?" I asked myself, staring at the script and pile of headshots.

The wheels were moving. Cher had sent a memo over with the rundown. My agent was a miracle worker. All the contracts were signed. The design teams were in touch with the writers and Cher. The studio's publicity machine was working overtime and the buzz was enormous. Interviews with talk shows were being set up and photo shoots had been scheduled. Bean Gomez accepted the director of photography gig and had passed on a huge film to take it. I'd been blown sideways by that wonderful nugget of information. Most importantly, Sean and the writing staff were creating magic. Everything was falling into place at warp speed. I wasn't even sure what I should be doing.

I still didn't know who the hussies were that Dick had hired onto the show, but I'd figure that out soon enough. If they were needed as extra protection, fine. If they were favors to his banging partners, no go.

"If anyone can make it work, you can, Cecily!" Man-mom called out from the kitchen.

I jumped. I hadn't even realized he was here. I had crappy Spidey senses. My house could be *filled* with flaming assholes and I wouldn't know.

"Thanks, Bill," I yelled back, organizing the piles neatly. My brain worked better when things were in order. Too bad my real life was in horrible disarray. Whatever. Wishing away reality was a waste of time. I had no time to waste.

The show was really happening. The excitement I felt was like nothing I'd ever experienced as an actress. The heartbreaking fact that I might not be part of the finished product tore at my soul, but maybe I could at least shoot the pilot and the first episode before I bit the dust. That was insanely selfish, but one could always hope. Sean would have to do a tremendous amount of rewrites to make it all work, but my brother was brilliant. My plan was to come back as a ghost. I could continue to have input on *Ass The World Turns*. Of course, I'd need a Demon to hang around and interpret for me and Uncle Joe. I made a mental note to put in a request. It was the very least my mother owed me.

"What are you doing here?" I asked Man-mom as I walked into the kitchen.

"Got you some food and needed to tell you Abe said he was going to stop by later," Man-mom said, putting groceries away.

"You shopped?" I asked, grabbing an apple and taking a bite.

My dad chuckled and held up a piece of paper. "Joe left a list—a very detailed one. I might not be able to see or hear my brother, but we can communicate through the written word. Not real fond of him drawing genitalia on my art, but Joe's always been a prankster."

"Wow. That's fantastic—not the genitalia part, the communication part." It was definitely interesting. I might not need a Demon interpreter after I died. If I could write to Sean and Man-mom, it would work.

"Apparently, your produce was hairy."

"Heard about that," I told him. "Did you replace all your expired food?"

"Yep," Dad said. "I tend to get a little absentminded when I'm creating art."

I just smiled. Man-mom was absentminded always. It was part of his charm.

"Would you like to talk about what happened this morning?" he asked carefully.

I didn't, but I would. "I got mad and accidentally set myself on fire."

The words were so absurd, I laughed. The reality of the situation wasn't all that funny, but it was laugh or scream. I'd done enough screaming lately.

Man-mom winced. "Okay. That sounds rather inconvenient... and dangerous."

"You think?" I tossed the apple core in the trash and grabbed a peach. "Not sure I can control it."

My dad sat down at the kitchen table. He opened up a box of Lucky Charms and scooped out a big handful. Meticulously separating the colored pieces from the beige ones, he nibbled on the blue moons. "Can Abe help you with that?"

I shrugged, sat down next to him and picked at the purple

pieces. Lucky Charms were more appealing than a peach. I didn't care about the carb count. I was on my way out soon. I was going to enjoy every unhealthy thing I could shove into my mouth. "I'm gonna go with a no on that. He was as shocked as the rest of us."

Man-mom arranged the yellow marshmallow pieces into a heart. "This was all because he burned down the lemon tree?"

I groaned. "No. That was what set me off. Dick was actually being very gentlemanly about it. I accused him of something, and he incinerated the tree instead of me. Once I got pissed, everything that's happened lately came crashing down around me and I lost it."

"What did you accuse Dick of?" he asked.

I froze. Shit. "Umm… I can't remember."

Man-mom gave me the side eye. For an actress, I was a crappy liar in real life. "The truth is a whole lot easier to remember than a lie," he pointed out, parroting what Uncle Joe had said earlier.

I sighed and let my forehead bang on the table. Honestly, it might not bother my dad a bit that Abaddon was doing the dirty deed with Lilith. My dad had moved on with Sean's mom. Also, I was a little unsure now if I was even correct. Dick's reaction to my accusation was kind of over the top. Before I spread the rumor, I was going to verify it. There was no reason to possibly upset my dad if I'd been wrong.

"What I said might have been off the mark," I admitted. "I don't want to repeat it."

"Fair enough." Man-mom leaned over and kissed my cheek. "You're a good person, Cecily."

"I'm a Demon," I reminded him. "Good and Demon don't belong in the same sentence."

"Wrong. Your mom was and is a beautiful and good woman. You're very much like her."

I bit back every ugly retort that sat ready on my tongue. Being like my mother was not a life goal for me. A change of subject was in order. I didn't want to burst into flames in my house. That would suck. I loved my house.

"When is Dick coming over?"

Man-mom stood up to leave. "Not sure. He said he was calling in a favor and would be back soon."

My heart beat like a jackhammer in my chest and a feeling of sadness washed over me. It was stupid. Abaddon had clearly taken me at my word and was finding a new Demon bodyguard to protect me. The thought made me want to cry. My guess was, asking him to kill me had been the straw that broke the camel's back.

What was wrong with me? I didn't like him. He didn't like me. We were a crappy fit. It was smart to go our separate ways. He was difficult to manipulate. Maybe the new bodyguard would be easier to convince to end my life. Life marched on even if it didn't go my way.

I sighed at the randomness of my thoughts. The past wasn't in my control to change. It was set. The future was mine to mold. My only concern was that Man-mom and Sean were spared. Period. Whichever way I got there was the way I would go. Right now, my elimination was the only way out I could see.

My gut churned when I truly thought about the reality of what I'd requested. However, the knowledge that I could have killed my dad and brother outweighed my fear. The sorry fact that I was going to be hunted the rest of my life by flaming assholes made my decision a no-brainer. I stared at my beloved dad and memorized the laugh lines on his beautiful face.

"I'm going to finish a painting," Man-mom said. "You okay alone?"

I smiled at him. "Yep, and you're right next door if I need you. Is Sean around?"

"Don't know." My dad cleaned up the cereal mess and put the box in the cabinet. Man-mom waggled his brows and grinned. "Said he had a date after the writer's session."

"Ohhh, he likes Georgia—one of the writers on the show."

"She's a terrific gal," Dad said. "Hope he doesn't screw it up. We're not the best in the relationship department."

"Word," I agreed.

After another kiss and an awesome hug, Man-mom left.

"Uncle Joe?" I called out, removing my contact lens so I could see him.

There was no answer. I really was alone.

I put my lens back in. Taking advantage of the break, I went to my room and pulled on some running clothes. With so much going on, a jog might help clear my chaotic mind. Granted, I could only run up and down the street since it was the only area I knew was safe, but it was better than nothing.

Cher was usually late and she knew Abaddon. If she showed up when he did, it would be fine. We could talk show business then, when she left, we could talk Demon business.

∽

WELL, TRUE TO FORM FOR MY LIFE LATELY, IT WAS *NOT* FINE—very little was going as expected.

"What the hell?" I muttered as I quietly closed the front door behind me. Staying hidden in the foyer, I took in the strange scene going down in my living room. Chill bumps popped up on my arms and a bad feeling settled in my gut.

Apparently, I was having a party and someone forgot to send me an invite. For a hot sec, I considered grabbing one of the twelve blowtorches I'd ordered. I punted that plan. I had no clue how to use a blowtorch and didn't have time to read the directions. Incinerating my house seemed counterproductive.

Cher had shown up and let herself in. This should not have been a problem. I'd hidden my battery-operated-boyfriend and everything incriminating.

Abaddon was also in my house, which also should not have been an issue. However, he'd brought a man and a woman with him. I was pretty sure neither was human. No Goat Eyes, but I could feel an enormous amount of power floating in the air. The man and the woman were stunningly beautiful.

The woman wore a colorful funky dress that I would definitely buy—even if it wasn't on sale—and looked like a supermodel. She had wild dark curly hair, amber eyes and legs that went on for days. The man was terrifying. He was the ridiculous kind of handsome like Abaddon. His eyes were more of a gray-blue and his hair was blond. His muscular build was evident in his jeans and black long-sleeve shirt. Both were basically too good-looking to be real.

I felt gross in my sweaty running clothes. Thankfully, my entrance had not been noticed. I spotted Uncle Joe behind the curtains. He gave me a covert thumbs up. This was a shitshow waiting to happen. I felt it in my bones.

My agent was in rare form. Her lined and bright red lips were moving a mile a minute. Her pink power suit was a size too small and she was teetering on her sky-high heels as she pled her case. The unfamiliar couple seemed a bit shell shocked.

"I can make you stars!" Cher told them. "With your looks, I can bag you a commercial in five minutes—a national one.

Trust me on that. Just sign on the dotted line and we're in business."

The woman tried not to laugh. "That's wildly flattering," she said, attempting to hand the contract back to Cher. Cher was having none of it. "However, I'm not an actress and have no desire to be one. I've got no talent in that department."

"Doesn't matter," Cher assured her, pulling a lip pencil out of her bag and relining her overly lined lips. "Three fourths of the idiots working in television today don't have as much talent as my pinky toe."

"Thanks, but no thanks," the pretty woman said again.

Cher needed hearing aids. She just kept on going. "Abe! Tell these people how good I am."

"I wouldn't know where to start, Mariah," Abaddon said dryly, shaking his head in annoyance.

"It's Cher now," she corrected him. "Although, I'm thinking about going back to Gaga."

"Is this a joke?" the mystery man inquired, eyeing Abaddon with displeasure. "This is why you requested our presence?"

Abaddon rolled his eyes and waved his hand. Cher was now frozen. She was as still and as silent as a statue. My stomach tightened. Her mouth was wide open. The lip pencil was clutched in her hand. It wasn't her best look.

Turning my agent into a statue didn't work for me. The time for hiding and spying was done. "If you hurt her, I'll set your ass on fire, Dick," I snapped, moving quickly to Cher and examining her.

The mystery man laughed. The woman shot Abaddon a surprised glance. My asshole Demon bodyguard simply uttered a few choice swear words and glared at me.

"You're going by Dick?" the man questioned, clearly amused.

"Zip it," Abaddon snapped.

"Everyone, relax," the woman said.

"Easier said than done," I muttered, carefully touching Cher to make sure she wasn't a stone replica of her former self. She wasn't. "What did you do to her?"

"She's fine," Dick said flatly. "As soon as we're done here, I'll break the spell."

"Nope, I don't trust you. Break the spell now and I'll convince her to leave. And, hi, I'm Cecily. I live here."

"I'm Daisy," the woman said. "Lovely to meet you." She had a Southern accent and really good manners.

"Gideon," the man said, staring at me with a perplexed expression on his face. "Are you..."

"Stop," Abaddon hissed. "Until we're alone, nothing will be discussed."

Gideon shot Abaddon a look that would have sent me running for my life. Abaddon just smiled and gave him the finger. These non-human people were nuts and really scary. At least they weren't on fire.

I closed my eyes for a moment. A large part of me wanted to kick everyone out of my house. While Daisy and Gideon were polite—Daisy more than Gideon—I had a feeling my life was about to take another weird turn. The thought was gas inducing.

Had Dick tattled on me and I was about to get in trouble? If that was the case, so be it. If Dick wouldn't end me, maybe Gideon would. He looked deadly and on the mean side.

"Unfreeze Cher. Now," I told Abaddon. "The hot mess I'm in has nothing to do with her. I want her out of here and safe. No disrespect to you guys," I said to the couple. "But Gideon is pretty terrifying."

Daisy swallowed back a laugh. Gideon simply raised a brow.

"As you wish," Abaddon said, waving his hand again.

A pop of shimmering red mist wafted through the room and I had to take shallow breaths so I didn't pass out. Magic made it difficult to breathe. As soon as the mist disappeared, my agent shuddered and came back to life.

"Holy crap," Cher yelled, looking around in confusion. "Lost my train of thought. Where was I?"

"You said you had to leave for a meeting with the set designer," I lied, wanting her out of here before something bad happened. "Right?"

Cher scratched her head and checked her phone. "Don't see that in my schedule, but it's not a bad idea. I feel like I was just having a conversation with someone…"

I glanced over at the couch. No one was there. No Dick. No Daisy. No Gideon. I almost screamed. Had I just had a hallucination? Did Daisy and Gideon exist? Was Dick even here? The only person I could spot was Uncle Joe hiding behind the curtain.

Wait. How could I see him? I had my contact in. Shit was going sideways.

"Umm… I don't know if you were talking to someone," I told Cher honestly. It was the truth. I wasn't sure anyone had been here. "I just came in from a jog."

She shook her head and chuckled. "I need some sleep," she said, yawning. "Been up for several days straight. Could have sworn I was just trying to sign two seriously good-looking people. I'm losing it."

"Join the club," I said with a forced laugh. I looked around again to see if they'd all hidden somewhere. Nope. The only person hiding was a naked dead man. "Do you need to lay down and take a quick nap? The guest room is open."

Cher slapped on some lip gloss. "I'll nap in the car on the way back to the studio."

"Please tell me you didn't drive," I said, pressing the bridge of my nose.

"Hell to the no! I hired a driver. His name is Bucky—hotter than the La Brea Tar Pits. I'd make my move if I wasn't married and he wasn't twelve."

"TMI," I said.

Cher cackled and handed me a folder. "Don't you worry your gorgeous head, Cecily. I don't have the energy to hit on Bucky. The sheer number of orgasms I've had signing all the contracts has put my dang cooter into traction, if you know what I mean."

"Oh my God." I groaned and hoped I'd imagined my guests. There was a fine chance they'd just gone invisible and were witnessing the conversation. "Let's keep discussion about your vagina off the table."

"Roger that," Cher said, grinning. "However, I do believe a good Big O would relax you. I say bang Abe. He has the hots for you."

"NO," I snapped in my outdoor voice as I grabbed Cher by the hand and dragged her to the door.

"You're right," she agreed, giving me a kiss on the cheek. My cheek was now smeared with gooey lip gloss. "Probably a bad move. Don't shit where you eat and all that."

"You should really stop talking," I said, opening the door.

"Holy crap! Almost forgot," she said, smacking herself in the forehead and almost knocking herself off her stilettos. "Slash reached out and wants to meet up."

"Slash?" I asked, confused. Had we hired someone named Slash?

"Your ex-husband! Slash Gordon. It's a brilliant publicity move. His people told my people that he still has a thing for you. Might not be a bad stunt."

Looking up at the ceiling, I sucked back a scream. "That is a hard no," I told her. "I was married to him for five minutes a hundred years ago and it was the worst five minutes of my life."

"I hear you," Cher said. "My second, third and fourth husbands fall into that category. Anyhoo, my guess is his people saw all the buzz around you and want to give his career a shot in the ass."

"Good luck to them with that," I said, gently pushing her out of the door and onto the front porch. "Tell Slash's people that it's not happening. Ever."

"You got it! I'll check in later. Gotta go flirt with Bucky!" She winked and teetered out to the waiting sedan.

I shook my head and grinned. Cher was nuts and I adored her.

I didn't adore Slash Gordon or Abaddon. Now, I just needed to go back inside and figure out what was real and what was not. I had a bad feeling the trio was still in my house. The fact that Cher had divulged horrifying things, was what it was. I had far bigger issues on my hands than my agent's active libido and my long-forgotten ex who wanted to hang out.

CHAPTER SEVENTEEN

I'D IMAGINED NONE OF IT. GIDEON AND DAISY WERE SEATED ON the couch. Abaddon was pacing the room. Daisy's expression was open and pleasant. Gideon's was reserved. He watched me with a puzzled look on his face. Dick's attitude sucked as usual. His scowl made me want to run after Cher's sedan and escape.

"You were married?" Abaddon inquired coldly.

I squinted at him. "Dude, that's none of your business."

"Keeping you alive is my business," he snapped. "So, you're incorrect, Cecily—again. Everything about you is my business."

I rolled my eyes. "If you hadn't made it abundantly clear that you hated me, I'd think you were jealous, Dick."

"Sounds like it to me," Daisy agreed with a grin.

Gideon simply stayed quiet. It was unnerving.

"I'm *not* jealous. I'd have to care to be jealous," Abaddon snapped. "I'm just verifying information to be able to protect you sufficiently."

"Thought you were booting the job," I said, sitting down on the armchair.

"You thought wrong," he informed me in a clipped tone.

Inside, I jumped for joy. On the outside, I kept my expression neutral. The fact that I was happy pissed me off. I was forty and behaving like a hormonal teenage girl with a crush on the bad boy.

"And you will complete the assignment I requested?" I pushed. May as well get it out on the table. My guess was, that was why Daisy and Gideon were here—either to talk me out of dying or to set some kind of punishment for asking. If that was the case, all three would learn that I was the boss of me—not them.

Abaddon refused to answer.

Not unexpected. We'd get back to that conversation later. "I'm so sorry," I said, standing up. "I didn't offer you anything. Would either of you like something to eat or drink?"

Gideon held up a hand and declined. Daisy smiled and shook her head. "No thank you. We're fine."

I didn't bother offering anything to Dick. If he wanted something, he could go get it himself.

Gideon leaned forward and rested his elbows on his knees. The man stared at me with such intensity, I wondered if I had something on my face.

Wait. I did have something on my face. Cher's freaking lip gloss. Quickly wiping it away, I sat back down and waited. If they had something to say, they could say it. Otherwise, this was going to be a very awkward get-together.

"Do you know who you are?" Gideon asked, still looking at me like I was some kind of bizarre science experiment.

"I'm Cecily Bloom," I said. If he wanted to play games, I was in.

Uncle Joe waved his hands at me frantically. I tried not to look at him. Revealing his presence wasn't part of the game. I was shocked I could see him with my contact in and I worried that Dick could too. Of course, when he darted out from behind the curtain and floated next to me with his balls at eye level, it was all I could do not to shoo him away.

Pretending was what I did for a living. I'd just do my damnedest to pretend my uncle's junk wasn't suspended in the air next to my face.

"Oh my gosh," Daisy said, stifling a giggle. Her eyes had gone wide and I would swear she was staring at Captain Nudeman. I didn't like that a bit.

"What?" I asked, a little ruder than intended.

Daisy fixed her gaze on me and smiled kindly. "Are you aware that there's a naked deceased man floating next to you?"

"I am. He's my uncle Joe. He's a nudist and he enjoys dancing. I'd greatly appreciate it if we just behaved as if he wasn't here. He's an innocent and very nice man, and I don't want him mixed up in this Demon bullshit. Am I clear?"

"We're not here to harm your uncle," Daisy promised, waving at the naked ghost. "Hello, Joe. I'm Daisy. I'm the Death Counselor. If there's anything you need help with, please feel free to ask."

"Ohhh my!" Joe said. "Aren't you a sweet thing! And no, I'm just fine, thank you. As Cecily said, please go on with your business and pretend I'm not here."

"Little difficult to do when there's junk blowing in the wind," Dick pointed out.

I saw red… again. Not the kind that made me want to ignite, but I could feel my entire body flush and a silvery mist began to swirl around me. Gideon appeared shocked and Abaddon stood ready to put me out if I blew up. Too bad he was the reason I wanted to explode.

"You will NOT insult my family, asshole," I yelled. "The naked body is a beautiful thing. Balls are nothing to be ashamed of. My uncle Joe, who also goes by Captain Nudeman, is the kindest and most lovely person I know. One more crack about his wrinkled testicles or being a nudist and I will take you out, Dick."

"Thank you, darling!" Uncle Joe said.

"Welcome," I told him, looking right at him trying while not to wince at his flapping bits. It would completely negate my argument if I gagged at my uncle's junk.

"Wait. You're a nudist like your uncle?" Abaddon asked, trying not to grin.

I wanted to punch the smirk off his face. I also wanted to kiss him, which made me think I was batshit nuts. "You wish," I snapped, ready to lose my shit. It was one thing to have a go at me. It was entirely another to go at my dead, buck-assed naked, sweet uncle. "And no, I'm not a nudist. I would not want skid marks on my furniture. I'd have to put plastic on everything and keep bottles of disinfectant everywhere."

I froze and replayed the appalling words I'd just spoken in my mind.

"OH MY GOD," I shouted. "I can't even believe I said any of that. Abaddon, you suck. You bring out the worst in me." I addressed Daisy and Gideon. "Please erase all of that from your minds. Or someone let me know if I'm capable of erasing thoughts and I'd be delighted to wipe that from your memories. It was heinous. My bad."

Daisy giggled. Gideon laughed out loud. Uncle Joe hooted and cackled. Only Abaddon was not amused. He was always pissed.

"Sorry," I muttered then looked around. "Can *all* of you see Uncle Joe?"

All three nodded, but my focus was on Abaddon. "Did you know he was with me at your house?"

Abaddon grinned.

I wanted to die. He'd heard a whole bunch of shit I didn't need him to hear.

"You know what?" I said, standing up. "This has been great. I'm done. I have a TV show to work on and I'm going to die soon. So, while it was nice meeting some of Dick's buddies, you should probably leave. Although, I will add that I'm shocked Dick has friends."

"Holy shit," Gideon muttered. "It's unreal. Can't believe I never knew. Spitting image."

I closed my eyes and reminded myself sternly that Daisy and Gideon had been pleasant houseguests. It would be rude to go off on them, but I was close.

"Done with the cryptic stuff," I said. "Who are you and why are you here? All of this supernatural crap is really starting to chap my ass. So, let's just get down to business."

The three non-humans exchanged glances.

"She's a fucking nightmare," Abaddon said.

I flipped him off. Daisy giggled again.

"And is she aware of who she is?" Gideon asked.

Abaddon nodded curtly.

"*She* is standing right here," I snapped.

Daisy elbowed Gideon. They were very obviously together-together. "Cecily is correct." She turned her attention to me. "As I said, I'm the Death Counselor. I'm also the Angel of Mercy. I believe Abaddon requested my presence to see if your uncle needed assistance moving into the light."

"He does not," I said quickly, then stopped myself. I glanced over at Captain Nude-man. Sadly, my eyes landed on his gray nuts. Quickly raising my gaze, I looked him in the eye. "I shouldn't speak for you, Uncle Joe. Do you need Daisy to help you?" I held my breath. If he wanted to go, I would not cry.

Actually, I would. I was hoping to hang out with him after I got decapitated.

"I'm quite content right now," Uncle Joe told Daisy with a smile. "I want to stay. And if you would like, I would be delighted to dance for you before you leave."

"Terrific," Daisy replied warmly. "I would like that very much."

Daisy was either seriously polite or a glutton for punishment.

"Excellent!" Uncle Joe said, floating to the floor. "I must warm up. Don't mind me!"

It was kind of difficult not to mind him. He was naked and doing squat thrusts to get himself ready to perform.

"And who are you, Gideon?" I asked.

"To you or in general?" he inquired smoothly.

It took all I had not to roll my eyes. However, it was very clear that Gideon was a badass of epic proportions. "Not to be rude, but you are nothing to me. We've only just met. So, let's stick with in general."

"I'm the Grim Reaper."

Well, that sure shut me up. I suppose Abaddon had taken me at my word that I wanted to die. Problem was, I wasn't quite ready.

"Where's your black robe and scythe?" I questioned.

Gideon scrubbed his hand over his face to hide his smile. He failed. "Not how it works, Cecily."

"So, you're just going to kill me with your bare hands?" I asked.

He was confused. Everyone was confused.

"No," Gideon said, giving Abaddon a sideways glance of annoyance. "You need to step in here, Destroyer. Now."

"Destroyer?" I asked. "Is that your nickname?"

Abaddon stared at me for a long moment. It was rude and I found it hot. I needed my damn head examined.

"My title," he said.

"Dick the Destroyer has a nice ring to it," I pointed out. "I'm a sucker for alliteration."

"You have wonderful lady balls," Daisy said with a grin. "I like you."

I took a small bow. "Thank you. Now let's get back to why the Grim Reaper and the Angel of Mercy are in my house, shall we?"

"Fine question," Gideon replied. "I have no clue. Would you like to field this one, Abaddon?"

"Cecily has extraordinary power. She manifested it today. She can't control it. While it appalls me to admit it, I need help. You owe me. I'm calling in one of the favors."

"Why isn't Lilith dealing with this?" Gideon asked.

"I would think that would be obvious," Abaddon replied flatly. "Some in Pandora's camp have learned of Cecily's existence. If Lilith showed up, everyone would know. Cecily wouldn't last five minutes."

"Call me crazy, but who are we discussing?" Daisy asked. "I've heard Lilith's name mentioned. Never Pandora. Who are they and how do they affect Cecily?"

I loved Daisy.

Gideon took Daisy's hand in his. "The Darkness is a matriarchal society run by two ancient goddesses—Lilith and Pandora. Lilith is who I called for Abaddon's assistance recently. I owe her now. However, it's far better than owing Pandora. The goddess defines the word viciously insane."

"Okay," Daisy said. "And how is Cecily involved in this?"

"Lilith is my mother—or rather, my egg donor," I said. "I've never met her. She took off the day I was born."

Gideon gave me a sharp glance. It was really none of the man's business to judge how I spoke of the Demon who bore me.

"That would have been for your safety," the Grim Reaper said.

I shrugged. "That's what my dad says."

"Lilith is a smart cookie," Gideon said with great fondness.

Daisy's amber eyes turned bright gold and narrowed to slits. It was scary. I'd been wrong to think Gideon was the more terrifying of the two. I considered leaving, but I was dying to know if the Angel of Mercy was about to kick the Grim Reaper's butt. Seemed like everyone had banged my mother at one time or another.

"Lilith's a past gal pal?" Daisy ground out.

Gideon grinned, clearly adoring her possessiveness. "No. She's my sister."

And the bombs kept exploding.

"Oh my God," I shouted, pressing the bridge of my nose. "One of my uncles is a dead nudist and the other is the Grim Reaper?"

"Apparently, yes," Gideon said, amused. "I didn't know of your existence until today. My sister has been very good at hiding you."

"Not good enough," I muttered.

"Crazy question," Daisy said. Her eyes were back to normal. "Why on earth would a mother leave and then hide her child? I'd sooner cut off my own arm than leave Alana Catherine."

"No choice. It upends the balance of power in the Darkness," Dick said, joining the conversation. "Cecily should not have happened."

My stomach plunged to my toes. Twenty years of therapy went down the drain.

"There's a reason I named you Dick," I hissed. "As soon as this conversation is over, you are dismissed from my life, jerkoff. I have a purple fire sword. There are also a dozen blowtorches on my front porch that I can use in a pinch. I'll take care of the flaming assholes. I don't need you. You can tell my mother to stay out of my life. She's had plenty of practice so it shouldn't be a problem. You can take your rude self back to the Darkness and keep banging your goddess, who you think is so awesome."

Gideon's mouth was open. Daisy's eyes were wide. Dick punched the wall.

"Here's the deal," I announced, focusing on Uncle Grim Reaper. "I'm an actress. I'm set to star in a TV show that I'm creating. It's the biggest opportunity I've ever had in my life. I would like to get it up and running and then I need a favor from you."

"Here we go," Abaddon muttered, punching the wall again. Chunks of plaster flew all over.

I hoped he broke his hand. And he might not know it yet, but he was cleaning up that mess before he left.

"A favor?" Gideon questioned.

"Right," I said. "I need you to kill me."

The Grim Reaper squinted at me in disbelief. "I'm sorry. What did you just ask?"

"I told you, she's a fucking nightmare," Dick growled.

"I'm not talking to you," I snapped at him. "And if you put another hole in my wall, I'm going to shove the coffee table up your ass."

Abaddon looked down at the floor. I would swear on my Goat Eye that the bastard was laughing. He wouldn't be laughing shortly when I made good on my promise.

Turning back to Gideon, I forced a smile. "Look, there are

only a few in my life who I love unconditionally—my dad, my brother and my uncle." I realized in a moment of complete and utter insanity that I'd almost added Dick to the list. To say that I was losing it was an understatement. Smacking myself in the forehead, I got back on track. "My dad and brother are still alive. I'd like to keep it that way. I almost killed them today by accident. The flaming assholes will kill them. I'm sure of it."

"What exactly are flaming assholes?" Gideon inquired, confused.

He too seemed to be amused by me. I didn't like it, but he was my best shot at biting it. My hope was that since we shared DNA, he would do it in a friendly way.

"Pandora's henchmen," Dick volunteered.

"Ah, I see," Gideon said.

"Do you?" I demanded. "Do you see why I have no options here? I didn't ask to be a Demon. I don't want to be a Demon, but I have no choice in the matter. However, I can protect the people I love. Hence, I need you to off me. Painlessly if possible. Are you in or out?"

"Enormous lady balls," Daisy said, staring at me with admiration in her eyes.

I really did like her.

"I'm out," Gideon finally said after staring at me for a long moment.

I rolled my eyes. "Fine. You're not in the running to be my favorite uncle. I'll simply do it myself after we get the show up and running."

"Good luck with that," Dick muttered.

I glared at him. "What is that supposed to mean?"

He sighed and met my furious gaze. "Your power came in. No one of your age and utter lack of experience should be able to conjure the fire sword. My guess is that there's very little human left in you now."

"Still didn't answer the question. Why do I need luck killing myself? I can just drive my car off a cliff. Boom. Dead. Done."

The Grim Reaper sighed and sucked his bottom lip into his mouth. "Do you prefer the truth or lies, Cecily?"

The question was absurd, but I realized I had to think about my answer. The truth lately was hideous. Lies would probably be comforting. However, my comfort was irrelevant when Man-mom and Sean's lives could be in danger if I was uninformed.

"I would love to say I just don't give a fuck," I said, running my hands through my hair and wanting to cry.

"Oh no, darling!" Uncle Joe said, floating next to me and smiling sweetly. "You must give a fuck. But only give a fuck about the things that light your beautiful soul on fire. You must save all your fucks for the magical things in life!"

"Umm… okay," I said, smiling at my batshit crazy naked uncle. "Thank you. I'll keep that in mind, Uncle Joe."

He nodded happily then went back to his warmup.

"Truth," I told Gideon.

Gideon examined me for a long moment. "If you have your power and can produce the fire sword, you're no longer human. Therefore, it will be very difficult to die—almost impossible to commit suicide."

I rolled my eyes. "I was born half human. My dad is human. I only have one Goat Eye."

"Goat Eye?" Gideon asked.

I took out my contact and pointed to my eye. "One Goat Eye."

"I see two," Daisy said politely.

I shook my head. "Nope. I only have one."

"Two," Gideon corrected me, snapping his fingers, conjuring a mirror and handing it to me.

They were correct. I now had two Goat Eyes.

"SHIT," I shouted, tossing the mirror and shattering it. "Oh my God... Wait. Can I even say God anymore? Am I going to get struck by lightning? I have two damned Goat Eyes and now I have seven years of bad freaking luck for breaking the mirror. This day can't get much worse."

"It can always get worse," the Grim Reaper pointed out.

"How?" I demanded, then quickly held up my hands. "Don't answer that."

"Gideon," Daisy said, putting her hand on his back. "Can you help Cecily control her magic?"

He nodded, then pointed at me. "I can. You'll still need training and you have to be open to letting me help you."

"Or?" I asked.

"Or we'll both end up as ash on the floor," he replied evenly.

"Seriously?" I shouted.

The Grim Reaper grinned. "No. I was joking."

"How about this," I ground out. "Do not joke. You suck at it."

The room went silent. Daisy closed her eyes and groaned. Dick winced and shook his head. Clearly, I'd overstepped. Apparently, the Grim Reaper thought he was funny and no one had the guts to tell him otherwise... until now.

I didn't care.

I rolled my eyes. "Look, if you're going to kill me for insulting you, just do it, dude. I'm not taking back what I said. Your joke sucked. For the most part you seem like a nice killer. Being with Daisy gives you bonus points in the nice department. However, I'm living on borrowed time right now. My only priorities are the lives of my dad and my brother. After that, I'd love to make my dream of having my own show come true, but that's second to my family's safety. If you can help me control my magic so I can decapitate flaming assholes, awesome. If you can't, then you're welcome to leave."

"Very badass," Daisy said with a nod of approval.

"Quite," Gideon agreed. "Take my hand, Cecily."

The Grim Reaper—my uncle—reached out to me.

"Is this going to hurt?" I asked casually.

"You just lost some of your badass street cred with that question," he replied with a raised brow. "And the answer is yes. No pain, no gain."

"Wonderful!" I knew I sounded sarcastic, but I needed some kind of armor for self-protection. I took the Grim Reaper's hand in mine. "Let's do it."

"Hold up. You owe me," Abaddon said.

I narrowed my eyes at him. "I owe you nothing."

"Not you," he replied dismissively, while staring at Gideon. "You owe me, and I'm calling another favor in."

"Another?" Gideon inquired, giving the Destroyer an odd look.

"Another," Abaddon confirmed, placing his hand over mine and Gideon's.

I had no clue what was going on. If Dick wanted to add to the pain I was about to encounter, so be it. His enjoyment of my agony could be my payment to him for watching over me these last couple of days. Demons seemed into owing each other favors. Once I could control my magic, Dick was free to leave.

Demons were sick in the head and horrible beings. I looked at Abaddon for a long moment. His beauty made me breathless and his heartlessness tore at my soul.

"Will this be fun for you?" I asked in an icy tone.

"No, Cecily," he replied.

I laughed. It was tinny and humorless. "I beg to differ. I've made your life hell since the moment you showed up. This will be your payback. Adding to my pain with the Grim Reaper must be a dream come true for you, Dick."

"He's not—" Gideon began, only to be cut off by a vicious hiss from Abaddon.

"Let's get this over with," Abaddon ground out. "Do not go easy. Make sure she can control herself. There's no time to be subtle or gentle."

Abaddon's hatred for me was clear… and heartbreaking. I wished I could despise him as much. Sadly, some strange part of me just couldn't. I was a stupid idiot of epic and embarrassing proportions.

Whatever. Maybe the pain I was about to experience compliments of the Destroyer would finally make me hate him as much as he hated me. One could hope.

"Do this. Now," Abaddon growled.

The Grim Reaper wasn't happy. He leveled a hard gaze at the Destroyer. "How long?"

"A day at most," Abaddon replied.

Gideon's lips compressed into a thin line. "Lilith has warded the area?"

"She has."

"It will hold?" Gideon asked.

"Until the end of time," Abaddon said flatly.

Gideon nodded to Daisy. She took Uncle Joe's hand in hers and led him out of the room. I was shocked she could touch him. Captain Nude-man was delighted by the Death Counselor/ Angel of Mercy.

"Time is ticking," Abaddon ground out.

The Grim Reaper eyed the Destroyer, clearly weighing the pros and cons. I still wasn't sure what the hell was going down.

"Backup?" he asked.

Abaddon nodded. "Already on the way. You owe the goddess and you owe me. I'd suggest you get to work, Reaper."

"The amount of power about to be unleashed will alert every Demon in the continental USA about Cecily. Lilith's daughter is a Goddess. Period," Gideon said. "You want to take that risk? If Pandora doesn't know about Cecily yet, she will shortly."

"Pandora already knows," Abaddon replied. "The stronger and more in control Cecily is, the better the chance of her living to see next week. Shall we get started?"

"As you wish," Gideon replied tightly. "I'll leave immediately after the spell has been cast. That might help tamp down the power surge."

"I'll owe you," Abaddon said.

"Let's just call it even," Gideon replied.

A smoky citrus-scented wind blew through the room and time seemed to speed up. My skin felt rubbery and my lips went numb. The Grim Reaper's eyes turned blood red and began to spark. The air in the room was heavy and thick. I managed my breathing by taking small shallow breaths. My head felt light and my body felt like it belonged to someone else.

Swaying on my feet, I willed myself not to scream when the pain started. I was a Demon. I had every plan to be the badass Daisy believed I was.

"Look into my eyes, Cecily," Abaddon instructed, taking my chin with his free hand and gently turning my head. "Connect with me."

"Why?" I gasped out, unable to look away. My ears rang and

it was difficult to focus. However, the horizontal silver pupils in Abaddon's eyes felt like a homing beacon.

"I'll make it easier. Trust me."

"I shouldn't trust you," I gasped out, doing my best not to pass out due to lack of oxygen and the spinning room.

The Destroyer tucked my hair behind my ear and smiled. "No, but you do," he said. "And you should. Keep your eyes on mine."

I nodded jerkily. It would take a tsunami to make me look away.

Again, I was an idiot.

The Destroyer wanted to watch my pain and enjoy it. Fine. If this was the way of the Demons, I would take it in and learn from it.

"Life is really simple, but we insist on making it complicated," I whispered brokenly.

"Confucius," Abaddon said.

"Correct," I replied. "If you're going to kick authority in the teeth, you may as well use two feet."

"Not a clue who said that."

"Keith Richards," I told him.

The Destroyer laughed. It delighted me to see him smile even though he was an awful person. Even awful people had their moments.

The air grew frigid as the Grim Reaper began to chant. The language was somehow familiar even though I didn't understand a single word. A sparkling black mist wafted through the room mixing with the scented breeze. It twisted and swirled. I wanted to touch it, but my body refused to obey my thoughts.

The pain began. It rolled in like an earthquake from Hell. However, it was not what I'd expected.

Not even close.

My screams came from worlds away. I could barely hear them. They came from the deepest and darkest part of my soul. My heart pounded in my chest and the blood roared in my ears. I begged the Grim Reaper to stop, but he didn't listen. I wasn't sure if the words I screamed made sense. Refusing to give up, I kept trying.

I had to stop it. It was all wrong.

I felt no pain at all.

The Destroyer had taken the pain from me.

All of it. And it was killing him.

Abaddon's body convulsed as bolts of electricity seemed to explode on his skin then wrap him in a deadly embrace. Tears of blood streamed from his eyes. Blood gushed from his mouth.

"NO," I screamed. "NO!"

The Grim Reaper had tried to correct my assumption. I hadn't listened. Never assume… It makes an ass out of you and me.

Abaddon had not wanted to watch me feel pain. It was the opposite. The Demon wanted to take the pain for me.

A fury I didn't understand began to build in my gut as I watched Abaddon suffer. Demons were right out of their minds, and I realized I fit in just fine. Closing my eyes took superhuman effort. However, once I broke eye contact, Dick could no longer take my pain. His body shuddered and he fell to the floor.

Raising my free arm high, I slashed it down to my side. The living room was now on fire. I finally had the Grim Reaper's attention.

"STOP," I shouted, furious. "You're killing him."

Gideon's brows shot up and he laughed as he snapped his

fingers and doused the fire. "Hardly. It would take much more than that to eliminate the Destroyer. Trust me."

"Easier said than done," I ground out as I dropped to my knees and checked Abaddon's pulse.

It was strong even though he looked dead.

With one last quick chant that made me feel like my internal organs had been gouged with flaming-hot daggers, the Grim Reaper finished.

"Done," Gideon said as Daisy suddenly appeared by his side. He backed away from me and in an explosion of black shimmering crystals, the Grim Reaper and the Angel of Mercy disappeared.

The Destroyer lay in a bloody heap on the floor.

"Shit. Shit. Shit. I give a fuck!" I yelled as I wrapped my arms around the beautiful Demon. I did not trust the Grim Reaper. I had no clue who in the hell I trusted right now. Uncle Joe's words about what to give a fuck about raced in my mind. "Hear me, Lilith—you sorry excuse for a mother. Abaddon lights my soul on fire. He *is* my magic. If you let him die, I swear I'll find you and make you pay. I'll also end your asshole brother, the Grim Reaper."

"Cecily, no," Abaddon choked out weakly. "Do not make a deal for me. Don't threaten those who rule. I'll be fine."

"Umm... you don't look fine," I snapped. "Who gave you permission to do that? I outrank you. Do not EVER do something like that again. Am I clear, Dick?"

A small smile pulled at the corner of his bloodied lips. "You're very bossy."

"You have no idea," I muttered, yanking the blanket from the back of the armchair and wrapping it around him. "When you told Gideon a day, what did you mean?"

"It will take me a day to regain my strength," he said.

"Are you worthless right now?" I asked, wanting to know exactly what we were dealing with.

The Demon squinted at me then shook his head. "You certainly know how to kick a man when he's down."

I rolled my eyes. "You know what I mean."

"I do," he replied. "The answer is yes and no. I'm at low power, so I can't defend you for a day, but I can call on those who can."

"The backup Gideon mentioned?" I demanded.

Abaddon nodded.

"We're right here," a female voice purred.

"At your service," another said with a giggle.

My body tensed. The voices were familiar. My need to electrocute something was overwhelming. Slowly turning my head, I did my best not to lose my shit.

They were blonde.

They were *beewby*.

They eyed Abaddon like he was lunch and they were starving.

I wanted to set both of them on fire.

If Abaddon hadn't almost died for me, I would have set *him* on fire.

However, the Grim Reaper had been correct. Things could always get worse.

Rhoda Spark—AKA Nip Slip—and Ophelia from *The Ocean is Deeply Moving* were standing in my living room. They'd clearly been the busty blondes who Uncle Joe had seen at Abaddon's.

Awesome. Not.

"*That's* the backup?" I asked, blowing out a pissed-off breath.

"That's the backup," Abaddon confirmed, right before he passed out.

The new wrinkle made me want to blow something up. I knew I could do it. The Grim Reaper had definitely helped me with my magic. Whereas before, I felt my power owned me, I now felt like I owned my power—not that I knew what to do with it, but I knew it was mine.

I just hoped being protected by two blonde, *beewby* bimbos would be as bad as it would get. I couldn't take anything worse than this.

CHAPTER EIGHTEEN

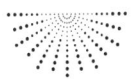

"What did you do to the Destroyer?" Ophelia spat furiously as her gaze went from the unconscious Dick to me

Thankfully, he was still breathing, but Rhoda looked perplexed as to why he wouldn't wake.

Ophelia, however, was pissed. The expression on her face was venomous and hostile. It marred her beauty and made her ugly. Even though I barely knew her, she clearly didn't like me any more than I liked her.

It was true that the pain Abaddon had taken was supposed to be mine. He'd crippled himself to absorb the excruciating side effects of the energy Gideon had given me so I could control my increasing powers. I still didn't understand why the Demon had done it. Why had he made himself vulnerable for me? It shot my theory that he wanted me dead right in the ass. Still, I hadn't made him do it, and I certainly hadn't done it to him.

"I did nothing," I said flatly.

Ophelia laughed derisively.

I electrocuted her.

She stopped laughing.

"Enough! That's not nice," Rhoda said, slapping out the fire on Ophelia and sounding somewhat sane. "We can't destroy each other! We're here to keep you alive, Cecily Bloom. Explosions are a terrible plan."

Nip Slip, for being a dingbat, had a point.

I eyed Ophelia dispassionately for a long moment as she eyed me right back.

"Fine," I ground out. "I will not set anyone on fire."

"Or electrocute anyone," Rhoda chimed in.

I shrugged, shaking off the sparks tickling my fingertips. "Or electrocute."

Ophelia flipped me off.

Dammit. I couldn't help myself. I wiggled my fingers and set her bleached-blonde hair ablaze. It felt fantastic. The smell was heinous, but the flames were lovely.

"For the love of everything evil," Rhoda shouted, tackling Ophelia and rolling her until the fire went out. "That was not nice, Cecily. I must insist that you apologize to Ophelia."

"Are you for real?" I asked.

Rhoda hopped to her feet once she was satisfied that Ophelia wasn't going to end up a pile of ash. "I am!"

I sucked my bottom lip into my mouth and debated my next move. Rhoda's nip had slipped again. She really needed a good bra. Since she was nice and had always been friendly when we'd run into each other, I decided to help a girl out.

"Your nipple is showing," I whispered.

"Whoops!" Rhoda squealed, tucking it back into her tiny crop top. "Anyhoo, we're here to protect you. If you set us on fire, we can't do our jobs."

"Obviously," Ophelia grumbled as she got back to her feet. "I believe I missed your *apology*, Cecily."

"Actually, you didn't," I replied sweetly.

Half of the blonde hair on her head was singed off. I winced. It was not good manners to incinerate people—though I was pretty sure the blondes were Demons—even if they were assholes. I was better than that. Dick had obviously called them in as backup, which meant they were on my side. However, I still wasn't going to say I was sorry. I was a crappy liar in real life, and I wasn't sorry at all. I'd happily flambe Ophelia again if she looked at me sideways. I knew Uncle Joe would be disappointed in me, but as far as I could tell, he wasn't here. Glancing around, I confirmed it. Hopefully, he was with Sean and Man-mom.

"So, you two are Demons, right?" I asked, moving on and changing the subject.

"Are you brain damaged?" Ophelia shot back. "Yessssss, we're Demons."

"Ophelia," Rhoda said in an admonishing tone. "No reason to be rude."

From what I could see, Ophelia didn't need a reason. "How old are you?" I asked them, noticing that Abaddon was coming to, but having a difficult time keeping his eyes open.

I wanted to get him into a bed so he could sleep and heal. The less time I had to spend with Ophelia, the better. It was bad form to maim my bodyguards—even I knew that.

"That's quite a personal question," Rhoda said with a giggle.

"I'm forty," I said, laying it out. I was done guessing and assuming. It had led me down a path of one bad decision after another. From here on out I was going to ask questions. Gideon might have helped me control my power, but I needed knowledge to use it—the more the better. Blonde Tweedledumb and Tweedledumber might have information that would help me.

"Five hundred," Ophelia informed me, scratching her eyebrow with her middle finger.

She was jonesing to be bald. The woman was a demonic trash fire begging to happen.

"Two thousand," Rhoda chimed in.

I wouldn't have guessed her to be the older of the two. She didn't seem all that bright or savvy, but maybe she was a better actor than I'd given her credit for. I nodded curtly as a thank you for answering my question. At the very least, they were experienced even if they both looked twenty. "And you can kick the flaming assholes' asses?"

Rhoda looked confused. Ophelia seemed perplexed as well.

"Could you be more specific?" Nip Slip inquired.

"Pandora's thugs," I clarified. It was abundantly clear I was the only one who referred to them as flaming assholes.

Both female Demons were silent. That didn't bode well. Had Abaddon picked them because he was banging them instead of for their skills? It wouldn't be the first time a director or studio exec hired his mistress, or in this case mistresses, for roles they weren't qualified for. I'd be asking him that shortly. No more leaving important questions unanswered.

"Umm... I think it best that we all stay away from Pandora's henchmen," Rhoda volunteered. "We should stay within the warded area until Abaddon is well."

"What she said," Ophelia announced, sitting down on my couch and making her rude ass very comfortable.

"Check the warded perimeter," Abaddon instructed, with his eyes still closed. "Concerned about the amount of magic used by the Grim Reaper."

A jolt of joy rushed through me. He was awake and talking. I took that as a good sign and tried to keep the worry out of my tone. "I thought you said it would hold until the end of time."

Abaddon nodded. "It will. Doesn't mean it won't need repairs here and there." He gestured to the blondes. "Get to it."

"Do we have to?" Ophelia pouted.

Rhoda looked similarly dejected. Neither of them wanted to leave him, and I couldn't help but feel a little irritated.

"Go. Now," Abaddon said weakly.

Rhoda and Ophelia both took their sweet time. They were messing with the Destroyer when he was down, and I wasn't having it. My life was always going to be in danger. However, the lives of my dad and my brother depended on the warded area. Not to mention, Dick—though it was getting harder to think of him by that name—would be in peril if the flaming assholes showed up right now.

"Move it," I snapped as my fingers began to spark and spit silver fire. "You do *not* want me to give you incentive since I'm not exactly sure what will happen if I do."

Both women hightailed it out of the front door.

"You." I pointed at Abaddon. "We need to talk."

"Worst fucking phrase in the English language," he muttered. "Help me up, please."

I did. I led the huge Demon to my bedroom, made him comfortable and tucked him in.

It was time to chat.

∼

Thirty minutes later, I was annoyed.

Abaddon was pissed.

I'd cleaned him up and made him a sandwich. He'd inhaled it. I made him three more and he'd made short work of those too. The Demon looked a whole lot better than he had a short time ago. That was good. The chat... not as much.

"Holy shit, Cecily," Abaddon said, pressing the bridge of his nose. "How many times can I answer the same question?"

"Sorry," I muttered, pacing the room and winding up for the next round of horrifying questions I needed to ask.

"The answer is no, and it will stay no," Abaddon repeated for the umpteenth time. "I'm not *banging* Rhoda or Ophelia. However, I find it curious as to why it would matter to you."

"We'll get to that shortly," I said. Since I was probably going to be dead by Monday, I had no problem getting honest. "And those bimbos are capable of protecting me?"

"They are," Abaddon assured me. "However, I think you're stronger than they are, at this point. I'll choose others next time. They're fine for now. I'll be back to myself by tomorrow."

The Demon crossed his arms over his wide, muscular chest and waited for more questions. He didn't have to worry. I had plenty more.

"Are you banging my mother?" I asked.

Abaddon exhaled a loud breath then rolled his eyes. "What do you think the answer to that question is, Cecily?"

"I don't know," I shot back.

"Actually, you do," he countered.

"Okay, fine," I snapped. "I'll concede that I might have been wrong in that assumption."

"Dead wrong," he said flatly. "I have not and never would even think of my goddess that way."

Outwardly, I didn't move a muscle. Inwardly, I had a party. And Abaddon was correct. I knew in my gut that he wasn't getting it on with my mother, but it was fantastic to have it confirmed. Now that I had the banging questions out of the way, it was time for the deep dive. "Why did you take my pain away?"

His brow arched. His head dropped back on his broad shoulders, and he stared at the ceiling. "Is it not obvious?"

He looked damned hot in that pose. My mouth went dry. "Nope."

"You need it spelled out?"

"I do," I replied, feeling every kind of vulnerable. I hadn't felt this nervous about a crush since I was a teenager on the set of *Camp Bite* and my brother's stunt double told me I was pretty.

Abaddon met my gaze. "Seriously?"

The intensity of his stare made me feel naked and very horny. So be it. Naked and horny was better than dead.

"Seriously," I said.

Yes, I had an idea where he was headed. No, I wasn't stupid.

However, he was a kagillion-year-old Demon with the title of the Destroyer. I was a former human with forty years under my belt who could get pissed and set myself on fire by accident. We didn't have the same pop culture references. We hadn't graduated high school at the same time. We didn't even live on the same freaking plane of existence. What I thought was obvious, might be incredibly wrong.

I heaved out a sigh and forced a polite smile. "To be fair, it's been a rough couple of days—I went to Hell, found out the Grim Reaper is my uncle and almost died a few times." I stopped talking and looked at the man reclining on my bed.

He was so very beautiful. And more importantly, he was good.

Abaddon was a good man—he was still an asshole, but the good guy part won out.

"Look, since I have an Underworld bounty on my head, and

I'm most likely going to bite it sooner rather than later, I'm gonna live on the edge." I took a deep breath and let it rip. I didn't need for him to make himself clear. I just needed to make myself clear. I was responsible for me. Period. I was a badass. "I might be having feelings for you."

The Demon's smile grew wide and his eyes sparkled. "Might?"

I bit down on my lips to hide my grin. The grin won out. "Yessss, Dick. Might."

"Come here," Abaddon said, patting the space next to him on my bed.

I walked over and sat down. His scent made me happy-dizzy and the heat from his body felt like home.

"I lied to you," he said.

I jerked back and prepared to electrocute the bastard. When would I learn? I sucked in the romance department. Granted, my entire family sucked at romance. I should have known better. "About?" I asked warily.

Abaddon winked.

I almost punched him in the head. I refrained since he'd already bled for me once. I wasn't a total monster.

"When we touched and you asked if I felt the tingle... I lied. I told you I felt nothing." He glanced away for a moment before his hooded gaze landed back on mine. His words melted me when he confessed, "I felt it."

I was glad I hadn't punched him. That definitely would have killed the mood. My lips quirked up at the corners. "Interesting."

"Very," he said with a barely disguised smirk. "It's quite rare. Never happened to me before, as a matter of fact."

"Again, interesting," I replied, feeling in over my head now that things were going my way. I wasn't sure if he was being honest, but I was *very* sure it was the first time it had happened to me. "What should we do about this development?"

Abaddon's sexy smile sent my girlie parts into a tango and made my tummy do flips. "What would you like to do about it, Cecily?"

I stared at the ridiculously gorgeous Demon in my bed. He was most likely going to shatter my heart into a million little pieces, but I'd never felt as alive as I did in this very moment. The Demon did something to my insides and my heart that I couldn't describe. It was like he'd set me on fire without any of the pain that comes with electrocution or incineration.

"Date," I blurted out. "I want to date you."

I was incredibly proud of myself. I'd come so close to saying bang instead of date. While I *definitely* wanted to bang the Demon, I didn't want to come off as a loose woman.

Abaddon ran his thumb over his full bottom lip. It was stupid hot. "Kiss me."

"Now?" I asked, slightly terrified. "I mean, you were bleeding profusely not even an hour ago. You should probably get some rest. I could make you another sandwich or some chili."

He squinted at me. "Chili?"

I shrugged and tried to play my idiocy off. "Umm... sure. I make really good chili."

"Noted," he replied with a grin. "You scared?"

The truth was easier to remember than a lie, I reminded myself. It might not be cool, but it was probably the way to go. "Yes. Terrified."

The Destroyer stared at me. It was as if he peered right into my soul. "Same."

"Bullshit." I shook my head. "You're like a million years old."

"Older," he replied. "And I've never been as scared of anything as I have been of you."

"Shut the front door," I said with a delighted giggle. "Not true."

"All true. I want to kiss you more than I want my next breath, Cecily."

The seduction happened in the silence of a few breaths as we stared at each other. My heart fluttered in my chest, and I could swear I heard bells ringing.

"I'm in," I whispered, leaning forward.

Our lips met, and hot damn, tingle didn't describe the incredible rush of pleasure that went through me as his warm mouth moved against mine. My palms splayed against his chest as he wrapped his arms around me, drawing me deeper into the kiss. My toes curled as I gave in completely. Then the chiming started. A ding-dong of sorts, that my lust-fogged mind couldn't comprehend.

I eased back and breathlessly asked, "Do you hear the bells?"

"It's the front doorbell," Abaddon said, sucking my bottom lip into his mouth and making me see stars.

"My front door?" I asked against his lips, trying to use my broken brain. All of my blood had clearly rushed to my hoohoo. I was ready to jump the Demon even though he needed to rest.

"Yep," he replied huskily, pulling me closer.

"Wait," I said, coming partially to my senses. "I should get that. Right?"

Abaddon groaned and held my face in his hands. "Yes. The answer is yes. Mostly because I can't actually do any of the many, many things I would like to do with you until I'm healed."

I laughed. "We're dating. Banging isn't permitted until date five."

"Good to know," he replied. "However, I have a stipulation for dating."

I leaned back and waited. If he wanted nonexclusive, he was barking up the wrong tree. "And that would be?" I held my breath and promised myself I wouldn't electrocute him if he was into polyamory.

"You can't get anyone to kill you," he said. "I will not get romantically involved with someone actively trying to off themselves."

My explosive sigh of relief would have been funny if it wasn't so real. "I can see how that would be a deterrent."

"Deal?" Abaddon asked, looking like he was going to fall asleep again.

"As long as we can keep my dad and brother safe, it's a deal."

Abaddon smiled and nodded as he closed his eyes. "Have to rest."

I kissed his forehead and pulled down the shades. Life had taken a big U-turn, and I was all in.

CHAPTER NINETEEN

"Who rings a doorbell?" I asked as I walked through the house and made sure nothing looked as if otherworldly creatures—like myself—had been hanging out, electrocuting people, casting spells and bleeding all over the place.

Nope. Everything looked incredibly normal considering what had gone down. The mystery visitor couldn't be Manmom or Sean. They had keys to my house. Uncle Joe could float through walls. Ophelia and Rhoda could poof. Gideon and Daisy could poof too. I saw them do it. After all the time I'd lived here, I wasn't close with any of my neighbors. Everyone kept to themselves. Maybe it was a delivery… or a flaming asshole.

"Shit," I muttered, pausing mid-step. "Would a flaming asshole ring the bell?"

The thought made my stomach cramp. If it was a flaming asshole, that meant Nip Slip and Ophelia were probably dead.

I shook my head and inhaled deeply. I was being ridiculous. They'd been chosen because of their power. Abaddon was not a dummy. And as much as I'd enjoyed electrocuting Ophelia, I certainly didn't want the *beewby* blonde dead. Plus, Abaddon would have to let a flaming asshole in. I was positive none of them were on the invite list.

"Coming," I called out as the bell kept ringing.

Peeking through the peephole, I laughed with an absurd amount of relief. What the heck was Cher doing here at 8 PM? And why was she wielding one of my blowtorches?

"Cecily," Cher yelled. "Let me in. Shit's not right."

My relief turned to panic at her words. Yanking the door open, I grabbed Cher by the collar of her pink power suit and pulled her into the house. Slamming the door and locking it, I jerked both of us to the ground.

"Speak," I said, freaking out.

"There's a Demon out there," Cher said, pointing to the door. With her left hand clutching the blowtorch, she reached into her pocket with her right and retrieved her lip liner. She proceeded to go to town. By the time she was done, she looked like Bozo the Clown with a blowtorch.

My stomach dropped to my toes and my eyes narrowed. "Demon?" How in the hell did my overly made-up agent know about Demons? She was human. "Have you been drinking?"

"Do I look drunk to you?" she demanded.

"Umm… kind of," I said with an apologetic wince.

"Fair enough," she agreed. "I've had a couple hard ciders and a Valium, but I'm not drunk. I drove over and didn't get pulled over once."

"Congrats," I said. "And there's no such thing as Demons."

Cher rolled her eyes. "LA is filled with vipers and Demons. Trust me on that."

"Vipers?" I asked, worried there was some other fucking species that I wasn't aware of.

"Hell to the yes," Cher said, pulling a can of hard cider out of her Prada bag and popping the top. "I came over all excited to tell you that you've been booked on all the nighttime talk shows and I saw her."

"Saw who?"

"The fifty-five-year-old whore who banged my fourth husband before I took him to the cleaners for all he was worth," Cher said, chugging her cider. "Dina Slimeyassbitchface."

"That's a real name?" I asked, not following at all.

"Hell yes, it is. Saw her walking her damned poodles. Hooker's had so much work done, her face looks like a rubber mask. Almost firebombed the bitch. I actually liked Herb. Damn shame he couldn't keep his pecker in his pants."

I almost puked with relief. Cher hadn't been talking about a real supernatural event. "Wait," I said, making sure I had it right. "You mean a woman, not an actual Demon?"

Cher stared at me like I'd gone and lost it. She would not be wrong. "Not a real Demon, but if there was a real Demon, Dina Slimeyassbitchface would fit the bill," she said, reaching into her bag and pulling out another hard cider. "Drink this. You look like you need it more than I do."

Shit. I needed to get Cher out of here. The chance of Nip Slip and Ophelia the mega-bitch coming back soon was high. I might be tempted to electrocute Ophelia again, and I didn't want Cher in the middle of a magical shitshow. However, if she left, there was a good possibility she would use one of my multiple blowtorches on Dina Slimeyassbitchface. That could land my agent in jail. I didn't need that. If I lived, we had a show to do. Even if I didn't, there was still a show to do.

"Cher," I said, trying to gauge how wasted she was. Her eyes were not right. There was no way she was driving anywhere. However, I knew of a fabulous babysitter. "Sean wants you to pop over and read the new script. It's perfect that you stopped by! You want to go now?"

Cher sucked back the cider intended for me then belched. "Sure do!"

"Great," I said, grabbing my phone and texting my brother that Cher was coming over, and that I needed Cher, Man-mom and him to stay in the house until I gave the all clear. "Let's just walk you on over and—"

And that's when my bodyguard poofed back into my living room, screaming like the world was about to blow up. Nip Slip had paled to the point she looked like she was about to pass out. "It's her," she hissed. "We have to kill her."

Cher was flabbergasted, but tried to go with the flow. "Where did she come from?"

"Back door," I lied with a wince.

Cher nodded and fired up the blowtorch. "I got it! We talking about Dina Slimeyassbitchface?"

"Who?" Rhoda asked, confused.

"Yes," I chimed in, opening up the front door and pushing Cher out of it. "She's next door at Sean's. Haul ass over there."

I blanched when I saw Ophelia outside on my front walkway. She was missing an arm and a leg, and was bleeding profusely. "Help me," she begged.

"What the FUCK?" Cher bellowed. "Did Dina Slimeyassbitchface do this to you?"

"Help me," Ophelia choked out. "She lies."

"Oh, I know she lies," Cher said, pulling a pair of night-vision goggles out of her purse and putting them on. "Dina Slimeyassbitchface is a lying sack of shit. I will avenge you, bleeding lady. Do not worry!"

"Oh my God," I muttered, freaking out. "This is not happening."

"End her," Nip Slip snarled from behind me. "She's the one who betrayed you, Cecily Bloom. Kill her now. Scum like her does not deserve to live."

"Wait," Cher said, wildly confused. "So, Dina Slimeyass-bitchface isn't who we're after?"

Something felt way the heck off here. I backed away from both Nip Slip and the bloody Ophelia. Grabbing the blowtorch from Cher, I situated myself on my front lawn where I could see both of my Demonic bodyguards. Sadly, Cher was shortly going to need more therapy than normal. Getting her out of here wasn't an option.

"Stay behind me," I ordered, shoving the tiny woman out of harm's way then letting my gaze bounce between the two Demons who were supposed to be protecting me. "Explain what's going on."

"She let Demons in," Rhoda hissed, pointing at the barely alive Ophelia.

"No," Ophelia choked out.

"Yes," Rhoda shouted. "She opened the ward right up and invited them in. I stopped her. I saved you. I'm a hero!"

"Interesting," I said, feeling my anger well up.

I didn't need a blowtorch. I *was* a damned blowtorch. "So, you're saying Ophelia invited flaming assholes inside the warded area?"

"Yes," Rhoda said.

"And they came in?" I inquired, holding back my fury with effort.

"They did," Rhoda assured me. "Came right in. I killed all of them then had to fight off Ophelia. She did her best to feed me to the animals."

"No. No," Ophelia whispered. "No."

"Yes," Rhoda said. "End her, Cecily Bloom. It's your right."

I nodded and walked over to Ophelia. Keeping my back to Nip Slip, I squatted down and stared at the blonde bitch. "I believe you," I whispered. My mother had warded the area. From what Abaddon had told me, no one but him was allowed to choose which Demons were permitted inside—not Rhoda, and certainly not Ophelia.

No bad Demons had gotten inside the ward... No. That was incorrect. Rhoda Spark was a very bad Demon and a brilliant actress. She was also about to go down. Now to figure out what to do with her...

"MOTHERFUCKER," Cher bellowed as she dove for a blowtorch and fired it up. "That's my producer. Nobody messes with my business!"

My chest tightened to the point of pain as I watched Rhoda drag the defenseless Abaddon to the front porch by his hair. His furious grunt of pain as she pressed a dagger into his neck filled me with rage.

The purple fire sword burst from my hand. "Let him go now before I take your head off."

I gasped as she slit his throat and thick blood oozed from the wound, so he couldn't speak. His gaze was focused on me as he clutched his neck.

This was my fault. He'd taken my pain, and now he couldn't defend himself against one of his stupid underlings. The traitorous Demon laughed as she held him tightly to her body. Her unhinged cackle would stay with me for an eternity.

"You want your Demon?" Nip Slip reveled in the power she held over Abaddon in his weakened state. "He'll live for now, but only if you stay back. If you don't, I'll make sure his soul never sees the light of this realm ever again."

"Move away from him and you might live," I ground out.

She rolled her eyes. "You're playing out of your league,

Baby Demon. If you want him, you'll have to come after him. He'll be hanging out with Pandora until then."

I felt as if my heart was being ripped from my chest. "I'll find you, and I will make you pay for this."

"See ya," she snarled. "Wouldn't wanna be ya, Cecily Bloom."

And on that horrifying note, Rhoda vanished with the Demon I loved.

"Jesus Christ!" Cher shouted, kicking off her heels and sprinting over to Ophelia. "Hang on, Demon. I've got you."

I squinted at my agent certain I'd just heard her wrong. "What did you call Ophelia?"

Cher rolled her eyes and removed her hot-pink jacket and her ivory silk blouse. "Gave this shit up centuries ago. Can't fucking believe I'm jumping back in."

"What?" I asked as the batshit crazy woman removed her bra. She was now silicone tits to the wind.

"Is the bloody one a bad gal or a good gal?"

"Good, mostly," I said. "Are you stripping?"

"Don't I wish," Cher grumbled as shimmering white wings burst from her back. "Gonna heal the Demon. And it might have been nice for you to have clued me in that *you're* a dang Demon, Cecily."

My mouth fell open. "What are you?" I whispered as my half-naked agent squatted down and gently touched Ophelia.

"Used to be a fucking Angel," Cher griped. "Gave it up but apparently, once an Angel, always an Angel."

"You can heal Ophelia?" I asked, as Sean, Man-mom and Uncle Joe came barreling out of Sean's house.

"Yessssss," Cher hissed. "Means I'm gonna have to be a working Angel again for a century, but whatever. Worse things could happen."

"Speechless." I watched the golden light emanating from Cher surround Ophelia. The Demon slowly healed before our eyes.

Ophelia gingerly sat up and tested her new limbs. "Where's Abaddon?" she demanded as she glanced around in a panic.

"Nip Slip took him," I told her. "Said he'd be with Pandora. Does that mean they went into the Darkness?" Fear gripped me tightly. Abaddon, with his power on the fritz, was a sitting duck.

"No," Ophelia said with a shudder. "They went somewhere far worse than the Darkness."

Her ominous reply increased my anxiety. "What's worse than the Darkness?"

The blonde Demon shook her head and let out a slow breath. "Vegas."

"As in Las Vegas?" I asked. "In Nevada?"

"Yes," she replied, still looking horrified. "Sin City is a favorite of the Underworld—especially Pandora."

"Huh," I muttered. Could shit get any weirder?

Cher, who was having a near religious experience at the mention of the city where dreams go to die, quipped, "Guess we're going to Vegas this weekend!" She put her bra back on and took a chug from another hard cider she pulled out of her bag.

"Thank you for healing me, Angel," Ophelia said, bowing her head to Cher. "I owe you."

"Damn right you do, Demon," she muttered. Then she turned to my brother. "Sean, you have a script for me? I can read it on the drive to Vegas. I'm damned good at multitasking."

Sean, who looked dumbstruck, or maybe was just seriously stoned, nodded his head.

"We're driving? Not poofing?" I asked.

"Driving," Ophelia confirmed. "A poof would announce our arrival. We don't want that."

"Got it. And just a heads up," I said. "Nip Slip dies."

"I'm down with that," Ophelia conceded.

"Works for me," Cher agreed.

My father, who'd been quiet up until that point, asked, "Can I make a suggestion?"

"By all means," I said, walking into my house and grabbing my car keys as my dad followed.

He retrieved a card from his pocket. It was black with a number embossed on the front in shimmering silver foil—it almost looked alive. He handed it to me. "Call this cellphone number," he said.

I cocked my head at Man-mom. "Why? Who does it belong to?"

"Your mother," he said. "I think it's time you met her."

I stared at the card. Under normal circumstances, I'd flush the card down the toilet.

The circumstances were not normal.

I didn't have to like the woman who'd given birth to me then left. I didn't have to respect her. However, I was in a seriously shitty position. If it was just me I was concerned about, I wouldn't call her.

It wasn't just me.

It was Abaddon, and I wasn't willing to lose him.

I understood the game. Pandora had stolen something I wanted. She planned to destroy me when I showed up to get Abaddon back.

That was the game.

I just didn't know the rules… yet.

However, I played to win. Always. I wasn't about to change my ways now.

Glancing down at the card again, I realized my hand trembled. Whatever. I didn't want the woman's love or approval. That ship had sailed forty years ago. I only needed her skill and expertise.

She owed me that.

She owed Abaddon that.

I dialed the number and held my breath.

As the Underworld turned upside down, so did the days of my life.

The End… for now

NEXT IN THE GOOD TO THE LAST DEMON SERIES

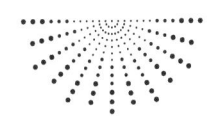

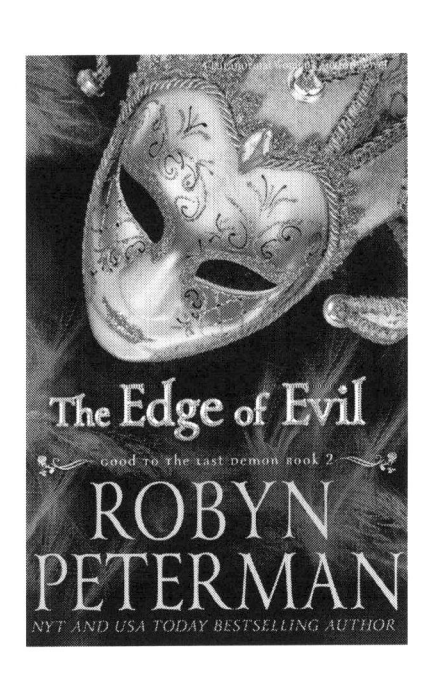

ORDER BOOK TWO NOW!!

What happens in Vegas, *slays* in Vegas.

With a show to produce and my career as an actress on the line, I really don't have time to die—especially violently. However, while that might not be on my agenda, it seems to be on other's.

Awesome.

Instead of acting in my latest endeavor, I'm playing the real-life role of Reluctant Demon Who Has To Save The World—or at the very least, the hot hero.
Fine. I'm always up for a plot twist or a re-write.

Scene One— Save Abaddon from the evil clutches of the hideous Pandora.
Scene Two — Don't die.
Scene Three — Avoid Pandora like the plague. I understand she has an evil box…
Scene Four — Do not die.
Scene Five — Possibly meet my mom, the woman who abandoned me as a baby.
Scene Six — Do Not Freaking Die.
Scene Seven — Go back to my non-deadly life and win a damn Emmy for *Ass The World Turns*.

Even though I'm living on the edge of evil, half insanity, half upheaval, I'm a pro and the show must go on.

As the saying goes, a bad dress rehearsal means I don't get dismembered on opening night. Or something like that.

It's showtime, folks.

ORDER THE EDGE OF EVIL NOW!!!!

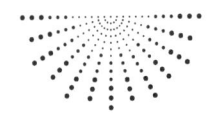

EXCERPT: THE WRITE HOOK

BOOK DESCRIPTION

THE WRITE HOOK

Midlife is full of surprises. Not all of them are working for me.

At forty-two I've had my share of ups and downs. Relatively normal, except when the definition of normal changes... drastically.

NYT Bestselling Romance Author: Check
Amazing besties: Check
Lovely home: Check
Pet cat named Thick Stella who wants to kill me: Check
Wacky Tabacky Dealing Aunt: Check
Cheating husband banging the weather girl on our kitchen table: Check
Nasty Divorce: Oh yes
Characters from my novels coming to life: Umm... yes
Crazy: Possibly

Four months of wallowing in embarrassed depression should

BOOK DESCRIPTION

be enough. I'm beginning to realize that no one is who they seem to be, and my life story might be spinning out of my control. It's time to take a shower, put on a bra, and wear something other than sweatpants. Difficult, but doable.

With my friends—real and imaginary—by my side, I need to edit my life before the elusive darkness comes for all of us.

The plot is no longer fiction. It's my reality, and I'm writing a happy ever after no matter what. I just have to find the *write hook*.

CHAPTER 1

"I didn't leave that bowl in the sink," I muttered to no one as I stared in confusion at the blue piece of pottery with milk residue in the bottom. "Wait. Did I?"

Slowly backing away, I ran my hands through my hair that hadn't seen a brush in days—possibly longer—and decided that I wasn't going to think too hard about it. Thinking led to introspective thought, which led to dealing with reality, and that was a no-no.

Reality wasn't my thing right now.

Maybe I'd walked in my sleep, eaten a bowl of cereal, then politely put the bowl in the sink. It was possible.

"That has to be it," I announced, walking out of the kitchen and avoiding all mirrors and any glass where I could catch a glimpse of myself.

It was time to get to work. Sadly, books didn't write themselves.

"I can do this. I have to do this." I sat down at my desk and made sure my posture didn't suck. I was fully aware it would suck in approximately five minutes, but I wanted to start out

CHAPTER 1

right. It would be a bad week to throw my back out. "Today, I'll write ten thousand words. They will be coherent. I will not mistakenly or on purpose make a list of the plethora of ways I would like to kill Darren. He's my past. Beheading him is illegal. I'm far better than that. On a more positive note, my imaginary muse will show his ponytailed, obnoxious ass up today, and I won't play Candy Jelly Crush until the words are on the page."

Two hours later…

Zero words. However, I'd done three loads of laundry—sweatpants, t-shirts and underwear—and played Candy Jelly Crush until I didn't have any more lives. As pathetic as I'd become, I hadn't sunk so low as to purchase new lives. That would mean I'd hit rock bottom. Of course, I was precariously close, evidenced by my cussing out of the Jelly Queen for ten minutes, but I didn't pay for lives. I considered it a win.

I'd planned on folding the laundry but decided to vacuum instead. I'd fold the loads by Friday. It was Tuesday. That was reasonable. If they were too wrinkled, I'd simply wash them again. No biggie. After the vacuuming was done, I rearranged my office for thirty minutes. I wasn't sure how to Feng Shui, but after looking it up on my phone, I gave it a half-assed effort.

Glancing around at my handiwork, I nodded. "Much better. If the surroundings are aligned correctly, the words will flow magically. I hope."

Two hours later…

"Mother humper," I grunted as I pushed my monstrosity of a bed from one side of the bedroom to the other. "This weighs a damn ton."

I'd burned all the bedding seven weeks ago. The bonfire had been cathartic. I'd taken pictures as the five hundred thread count sheets had gone up in flame. I'd kept the comforter. I'd paid a fortune for it. It had been thoroughly saged and washed five times. Even though there was no trace of Darren left in the bedroom, I'd been sleeping in my office.

The house was huge, beautiful... and mine—a gorgeously restored Victorian where I'd spent tons of time as a child. It had an enchanted feel to it that I adored. I didn't need such an enormous abode, but I loved the location—the middle of nowhere. The internet was iffy, but I solved that by going into town to the local coffee shop if I had something important to download or send.

Darren, with the wandering pecker, thought he would get a piece of the house. He was wrong. I'd inherited it from my whackadoo grandmother and great-aunt Flip. My parents hadn't always been too keen on me spending so much time with Granny and Aunt Flip growing up, but I adored the two old gals so much they'd relented. Since I spent a lot of time in an imaginary dream world, my mom and dad were delighted when I related to actual people—even if they were left of center.

Granny and Flip made sure the house was in my name only —nontransferable and non-sellable. It was stipulated that I had to pass it to a family member or the Historical Society when I died. Basically, I had life rights. It was as if Granny and Aunt Flip had known I would waste two decades of my life married to a jackhole who couldn't keep his salami in his pants and would need someplace to live. God rest Granny's insane soul. Aunt Flip was still kicking, although I hadn't seen her in a few years.

Aunt Flip put the K in kooky. She'd bought a cottage in the hills about an hour away and grew medicinal marijuana— before it was legal. The old gal was the black sheep of the

CHAPTER 1

family and preferred her solitude and her pot to company. She hadn't liked Darren a bit. She and Granny both had worn black to my wedding. Everyone had been appalled—even me—but in the end, it made perfect sense. I had to hand it to the old broads. They'd been smarter than me by a long shot. And the house? It had always been my charmed haven in the storm.

Even though there were four spare bedrooms plus the master suite, I chose my office. It felt safe to me.

Thick Stella preferred my office, and I needed to be around something that had a heartbeat. It didn't matter that Thick Stella was bitchy and swiped at me with her deadly kitty claws every time I passed her. I loved her. The feeling didn't seem mutual, but she hadn't left me for a twenty-three-year-old with silicone breast implants and huge, bright white teeth.

"Thick Stella, do you think Sasha should wear red to her stepmother's funeral?" I asked as I plopped down on my newly Feng Shuied couch and narrowly missed getting gouged by my cat. "Yes or no? Hiss at me if it's a yes. Growl at me if it's a no."

Thick Stella had a go at her privates. She was useless.

"That wasn't an answer." I grabbed my laptop from my desk. Deciding it was too dangerous to sit near my cat, I settled for the love seat. The irony of the piece of furniture I'd chosen didn't escape me.

"I think she should wear red," I told Thick Stella, who didn't give a crap what Sasha wore. "Her stepmother was an asshat, and it would show fabu disrespect."

Typing felt good. Getting lost in a story felt great. I dressed Sasha in a red Prada sheath, then had her behead her ex-husband with a dull butter knife when he and his bimbo showed up unexpectedly to pay their respects at the funeral home. It was a bloodbath. Putting Sasha in red was an excellent move. The blood matched her frock to a T.

CHAPTER 1

Quickly rethinking the necessary murder, I moved the scene of the decapitation to the empty lobby of the funeral home. It would suck if I had to send Sasha to prison. She hadn't banged Damien yet, and everyone was eagerly awaiting the sexy buildup—including me. It was the fourth book in the series, and it was about time they got together. The sexual tension was palpable.

"What in the freaking hell?" I snapped my laptop shut and groaned. "Sasha doesn't have an ex-husband. I can't do this. I've got nothing." Where was my muse hiding? I needed the elusive imaginary idiot if I was going to get any writing done. "Chauncey, dammit, where are you?"

"My God, you're loud, Clementine," a busty, beautiful woman dressed in a deep purple Regency gown said with an eye roll.

She was seated on the couch next to Thick Stella, who barely acknowledged her. My cat attacked strangers and friends. Not today. My fat feline simply glanced over at the intruder and yawned. The cat was a traitor.

Forget the furry betrayer. How in the heck did the woman get into my house—not to mention my office—without me seeing her enter? For a brief moment, I wondered if she'd banged my husband too but pushed the sordid thought out of my head. She looked to be close to thirty—too old for the asshole.

"Who are you?" I demanded, holding my laptop over my head as a weapon.

If I threw it and it shattered, I would be screwed. I couldn't remember the last time I'd backed it up. If I lost the measly, somewhat disjointed fifty thousand words I'd written so far, I'd have to start over. That wouldn't fly with my agent or my publisher.

CHAPTER 1

"Don't be daft," the woman replied. "It's rather unbecoming. May I ask a question?"

"No, you may not," I shot back, trying to place her.

She was clearly a nutjob. The woman was rolling up on thirty but had the vernacular of a seventy-year-old British society matron. She was dressed like she'd walked off the set of a film starring Emma Thompson. Her blonde hair shone to the point of absurdity and was twisted into an elaborate up-do. Wispy tendrils framed her perfectly heart-shaped face. Her sparkling eyes were lavender, enhanced by the over-the-top gown she wore.

Strangely, she was vaguely familiar. I just couldn't remember how I knew her.

"How long has it been since you attended to your hygiene?" she inquired.

Putting my laptop down and picking up a lamp, I eyed her. I didn't care much for the lamp or her question. I had been thinking about Marie Condo-ing my life, and the lamp didn't bring me all that much joy. If it met its demise by use of self-defense, so be it. "I don't see how that's any of your business, lady. What I'd suggest is that you leave. Now. Or else I'll call the police. Breaking and entering is a crime."

She laughed. It sounded like freaking bells. Even though she was either a criminal or certifiable, she was incredibly charming.

"Oh dear," she said, placing her hand delicately on her still heaving, milky-white bosom. "You are so silly. The constable knows quite well that I'm here. He advised me to come."

"The constable?" I asked, wondering how far off her rocker she was.

She nodded coyly. "Most certainly. We're all terribly concerned."

CHAPTER 1

I squinted at her. "About my hygiene?"

"That, amongst other things," she confirmed. "Darling girl, you are not an ace of spades or, heaven forbid, an adventuress. Unless you want to be an ape leader, I'd recommend bathing."

"Are you right in the head?" I asked, wondering where I'd left my damn cell phone. It was probably in the laundry room. I was going to be murdered by a nutjob, and I'd lost my chance to save myself because I'd been playing Candy Jelly Crush. The headline would be horrifying—*Homeless-looking, Hygiene-free Paranormal Romance Author Beheaded by Victorian Psycho*.

If I lived through the next hour, I was deleting the game for good.

"I think it would do wonders for your spirit if you donned a nice tight corset and a clean chemise," she suggested, skillfully ignoring my question. "You must pull yourself together. Your behavior is dicked in the nob."

I sat down and studied her. My about-to-be-murdered radar relaxed a tiny bit, but I kept the lamp clutched tightly in my hand. My gut told me she wasn't going to strangle me. Of course, I could be mistaken, but Purple Gal didn't seem violent —just bizarre. Plus, the lamp was heavy. I could knock her ladylike ass out with one good swing.

How in the heck did I know her? College? Grad School? The grocery store? At forty-two, I'd met a lot of people in my life. Was she with the local community theater troop? I was eighty-six percent sure she wasn't here to off me. However, I'd been wrong about life-altering events before—like not knowing my husband was boffing someone young enough to have been our daughter.

"What language are you speaking?" I spotted a pair of scissors on my desk. If I needed them, it was a quick move to grab

CHAPTER 1

them. I'd never actually killed anyone except in fictitious situations, but there was a first time for everything.

Pulling an embroidered lavender hankey from her cleavage, she clutched it and twisted it in her slim fingers. "Clementine, *you* should know."

"I'm at a little disadvantage here," I said, fascinated by the batshit crazy woman who'd broken into my home. "You seem to know my name, but I don't know yours."

And that was when the tears started. Hers. Not mine.

"Such claptrap. How very unkind of you, Clementine," she burst out through her stupidly attractive sobs.

It was ridiculous how good the woman looked while crying. I got all blotchy and red, but not the mystery gal in purple. She grew even more lovely. It wasn't fair. I still had no clue what the hell she was talking about, but on the off chance she might throw a tantrum if I asked more questions, I kept my mouth shut.

And yes, she had a point, but my *hygiene* was none of her damn business. I couldn't quite put my finger on the last time I'd showered. If I had to guess, it was probably in the last five to twelve days. I was on a deadline for a book. To be more precise, I was late for my deadline on a book. I didn't exactly have time for personal sanitation right now.

And speaking of deadlines…

"How about this?" My tone was excessively polite. I almost laughed. The woman had illegally entered my house, and I was behaving like she was a guest. "I'll take a shower later today after I get through a few pivotal chapters. Right now, you should leave so I can work."

"Yes, of course," she replied, absently stroking Fat Stella, who purred. If I'd done that, I would be minus a finger. "It would be dreadfully sad if you were under the hatches."

CHAPTER 1

I nodded. "Right. That would, umm… suck."

The woman in purple smiled. It was radiant, and I would have sworn I heard birds happily chirping. I was losing it.

"Excellent," she said, pulling a small periwinkle velvet bag from her cleavage. I wondered what else she had stored in there and hoped there wasn't a weapon. "I shall leave you with two gold coins. While the Grape Nuts were tasty, I would prefer that you purchase some Lucky Charms. I understand they are magically delicious."

"It was you?" I asked, wildly relieved that I hadn't been sleep eating. I had enough problems at the moment. Gaining weight from midnight dates with cereal wasn't on the to-do list.

"It was," she confirmed, getting to her feet and dropping the coins into my hand. "The consistency was quite different from porridge, but I found it tasty—very crunchy."

"Right… well… thank you for putting the bowl in the sink." Wait. Why the hell was I thanking her? She'd wandered in and eaten my Grape Nuts.

"You are most welcome, Clementine," she said with a disarming smile that lit up her unusual eyes. "It was lovely finally meeting you even if your disheveled outward show is entirely astonishing."

I was reasonably sure I had just been insulted by the cereal lover, but it was presented with excellent manners. However, she did answer a question. We hadn't met. I wasn't sure why she seemed familiar. The fact that she knew my name was alarming.

"Are you a stalker?" I asked before I could stop myself.

I'd had a few over the years. Being a *New York Times* bestselling author was something I was proud of, but it had come with a little baggage here and there. Some people seemed to

CHAPTER 1

have difficulty discerning fiction from reality. If I had to guess, I'd say Purple Gal might be one of those people.

I'd only written one Regency novel, and that had been at the beginning of my career, before I'd found my groove in paranormal romance. I was way more comfortable writing about demons and vampires than people dressed in top hats and hoopskirts. Maybe the crazy woman had read my first book. It hadn't done well, and for good reason. It was over-the-top bad. I'd blocked the entire novel out of my mind. Live and learn. It had been my homage to Elizabeth Hoyt well over a decade ago. It had been clear to all that I should leave Regency romance to the masters.

"Don't be a Merry Andrew," the woman chided me. "Your bone box is addled. We must see to it at once. I shall pay a visit again soon."

The only part of her gibberish I understood was that she thought she was coming back. Note to self—change all the locks on the doors. Since it wasn't clear if she was packing heat in her cleavage, I just smiled and nodded.

"Alrighty then…" I was unsure if I should walk her to the door or if she would let herself out. Deciding it would be better to make sure she actually left instead of letting her hide in my pantry to finish off my cereal, I gestured to the door. "Follow me."

Thick Stella growled at me. I was so tempted to flip her off but thought it might earn another lecture from Purple Gal. It was more than enough to be lambasted for my appearance. I didn't need my manners picked apart by someone with a tenuous grip on reality.

My own grip was dubious as it was.

"You might want to reconsider breaking into homes," I said, holding the front door open. "It could end badly—for you."

CHAPTER 1

Part of me couldn't believe that I was trying to help the nutty woman out, but I couldn't seem to stop myself. I kind of liked her.

"I'll keep that in mind," she replied as she sauntered out of my house into the warm spring afternoon. "Remember, Clementine, there is always sunshine after the rain."

As she made her way down the long sunlit, tree-lined drive, she didn't look back. It was disturbingly like watching the end of a period movie where the heroine left her old life behind and walked proudly toward her new and promising future.

Glancing around for a car, I didn't spot one. Had she left it parked on the road so she could make a clean getaway after she'd bludgeoned me? Had I just politely escorted a murderer out of my house?

Had I lost it for real?

Probably.

As she disappeared from sight, I felt the weight of the gold coins still clutched in my hand. Today couldn't get any stranger.

At least, I hoped not.

Opening my fist to examine the coins, I gasped. "What in the heck?"

There was nothing in my hand.

Had I dropped them? Getting down on all fours, I searched. Thick Stella joined me, kind of—more like watched me as I crawled around and wondered if anything that had just happened had actually happened.

"Purple Gal gave me coins to buy Lucky Charms," I told my cat, my search now growing frantic. "You saw her do it. Right? She sat next to you. And you didn't attack her. *Right?*"

Thick Stella simply stared at me. What did I expect? If my cat answered me, I'd have to commit myself. That option

CHAPTER 1

might still be on the table. Had I just imagined the entire exchange with the strange woman? Should I call the cops?

"And tell them what?" I asked, standing back up and locking the front door securely. "That a woman in a purple gown broke in and ate my cereal while politely insulting my hygiene? Oh, and she left me two gold coins that disappeared in my hand as soon as she was out of sight? That's not going to work."

I'd call the police if she came back, since I wasn't sure she'd been here at all. She hadn't threatened to harm me. Purple Gal had been charming and well-mannered the entire time she'd badmouthed my cleanliness habits. And to be quite honest, real or not, she'd made a solid point. I could use a shower.

Maybe four months of wallowing in self-pity and only living inside the fictional worlds I created on paper had taken more of a toll than I was aware of. Getting lost in my stories was one of my favorite things to do. It had saved me more than once over the years. It was possible that I'd let it go too far. Hence, the Purple Gal hallucination.

Shit.

First things first. Delete Candy Jelly Crush. Getting rid of the white noise in my life was the first step to… well, the first step to something.

I'd figure it out later.

HIT HERE TO ORDER THE WRITE HOOK!!!!!

ROBYN'S BOOK LIST

(IN CORRECT READING ORDER)

HOT DAMNED SERIES
Fashionably Dead
Fashionably Dead Down Under
Hell on Heels
Fashionably Dead in Diapers
A Fashionably Dead Christmas
Fashionably Hotter Than Hell
Fashionably Dead and Wed
Fashionably Fanged
Fashionably Flawed
A Fashionably Dead Diary
Fashionably Forever After
Fashionably Fabulous
A Fashionable Fiasco
Fashionably Fooled
Fashionably Dead and Loving It
Fashionably Dead and Demonic
The Oh My Gawd Couple

GOOD TO THE LAST DEATH SERIES
It's a Wonderful Midlife Crisis
Whose Midlife Crisis Is It Anyway?
A Most Excellent Midlife Crisis
My Midlife Crisis, My Rules
You Light Up My Midlife Crisis
It's A Matter of Midlife and Death
The Facts Of Midlife
It's A Hard Knock Midlife

MY SO-CALLED MYSTICAL MIDLIFE SERIES
The Write Hook
You May Be Write
All The Write Moves
My Big Fat Hairy Wedding

SHIFT HAPPENS SERIES
Ready to Were
Some Were in Time
No Were To Run
Were Me Out
Were We Belong

MAGIC AND MAYHEM SERIES
Switching Hour
Witch Glitch
A Witch in Time
Magically Delicious
A Tale of Two Witches
Three's A Charm
Switching Witches
You're Broom or Mine?

The Bad Boys of Assjacket
The Newly Witch Game
Witches In Stitches

SEA SHENANIGANS SERIES
Tallulah's Temptation
Ariel's Antics
Misty's Mayhem
Petunia's Pandemonium
Jingle Me Balls

A WYLDE PARANORMAL SERIES
Beauty Loves the Beast

HANDCUFFS AND HAPPILY EVER AFTERS SERIES
How Hard Can it Be?
Size Matters
Cop a Feel

If after reading all the above you are still wanting more adventure and zany fun, read *Pirate Dave and His Randy Adventures*, the romance novel budding novelist Rena helped wicked Evangeline write in *How Hard Can It Be?*

Warning: Pirate Dave Contains Romance Satire, Spoofing, and Pirates with Two Pork Swords.

NOTE FROM THE AUTHOR

If you enjoyed reading *As The Underworld Turns*, please consider leaving a positive review or rating on the site where you purchased it. Reader reviews help my books continue to be valued by resellers and help new readers make decisions about reading them.

You are the reason I write these stories and I sincerely appreciate each of you!

Many thanks for your support,
~ Robyn Peterman

Want to hear about my new releases?
Visit https://robynpeterman.com/newsletter/ and join my mailing list!

ABOUT ROBYN PETERMAN

Robyn Peterman writes because the people inside her head won't leave her alone until she gives them life on paper. Her addictions include laughing really hard with friends, shoes (the expensive kind), Target, Coke (the drink not the drug LOL) with extra ice in a Yeti cup, bejeweled reading glasses, her kids, her super-hot hubby and collecting stray animals.

A former professional actress with Broadway, film and T.V. credits, she now lives in the South with her family and too many animals to count.

Writing gives her peace and makes her whole, plus having a job where she can work in sweatpants works really well for her.